BACK
In The
GAME

OTHER TITLES BY CHARLES HOLDEFER

Apology for Big Rod
The Contractor
Nice

CHARLES HOLDEFER

BACK
In The
GAME

THE PERMANENT PRESS
Sag Harbor, NY 11963

Portions of this book appeared, in different form, in the *New England Review, Bread Loaf Quarterly, Yellow Silk,* and *Iowa Summer Writing Festival Anthology.*

For information, address:
  The Permanent Press
  4170 Noyac Road
  Sag Harbor, NY 11963
  www.thepermanentpress.com

Library of Congress Cataloging-in-Publication Data

  Holdefer, Charles —
    Back in the game / Charles Holdefer.
        p. cm.
    ISBN 978-1-57962-265-7
        1. Teachers—Fiction. 2. Country life—Fiction. 3. Friendship—Fiction. 4. Adultery—Fiction. I. Title.

  PS3558.O347746B33 2012
  813'.54—dc23   2012004250

Printed in the United States of America.

For Rosalie N. Riglin
(1921–2006)
writer

ACKNOWLEDGEMENTS

Thanks to Martin and Judith Shepard, who still believe in literary fiction.

Special thanks to Anna Lipinska, Geoff Pitcher, Tom and Kathy Holdefer, Curtis Smith, Joëlle Bonnevin, Jonathan Harrington, and Room 24 OC.

And he asked him, What is thy name?
And he answered, saying, My name is Legion:
   for we are many.
And he besought him much that he would not send
   them away out of the country.

MARK 5:9–10

Dancing

1

My first day as a respectable American again, I rode the school bus. I hadn't planned to be a rider, but my car broke down. The mechanic took me by the arm like a doctor consoling a relative; I felt sad at the sight of my machine bleeding oil; I caught the phrase *complete overhaul*, and we shook our heads. I couldn't afford to fix it. I was still waiting for my first paycheck.

So I rode the bus. I'd rented a farmhouse full of mice along the river, and that morning the bus picked me up and I joined the country kids. There were boys with fresh haircuts, girls in knee socks, chattering in groups as the bus bumped along the gravel roads. I watched the land drift by my window. Hillocks of alfalfa, patches of bare black earth; corn in the flats. There weren't many flats. Most of the countryside was rolling, feminine.

The bus pulled down a dirt lane and the riders fell quiet. They looked out the windows. This was the farm, I would soon learn, of Jimbo Snow.

It was a tiny house, with peeling paint, on an overgrown lawn. Half a dog protruded from under the front steps. The bus honked and the screen door flew open. There stood a thickset girl with glasses. She took slow steps toward the bus, cautious steps, as if afraid the lawn was full of snakes. "*Christine! My darling!*" cried a boy with scraggly sideburns, and all the children laughed. Christine came to the bus and made her way up the steps and immediately sat in the front seat next to the door, her back to the rest of the children. Some younger boys made smooching sounds and picked up the cry of "*Darling Christine!*" to the rousing approval of most of the riders. The white-haired bus driver did nothing. Then the boy with scraggly sideburns chanted "*Jimbo, Jimbo, Jimbo,*" the cry of a pep rally, and everyone's attention returned to the bus windows, and to the house. A shadow appeared in the door frame. "*Jimbo, Jimbo, Jimbo*" went the crowd, until a tall kid in denim emerged in the sunlight. He pounded down the front steps. The dog disappeared. The kid advanced across the lawn with long, deliberate strides, clenching a pencil in his fist and it seemed that he had a purpose, a definite object in mind, as he entered the school bus and faced the crowd, his head almost touching the metal ceiling. For a moment the riders hushed. His eyes glistened, his slim mouth fell open, but there was no sound: only movement, his chin, swinging back and forth. I couldn't help but stare with everyone else. The bus jolted, he sat down with Christine.

We continued down gravel roads, spewing dust, and soon came into town where we were let off at Legion Community School. On my way out I told the bus driver, "Catch you later," and he gestured for me to wait. He adjusted his glasses and clicked on a fat hearing aid that curled behind his ear.

"There, that's better," he said. "My name is Russell."

I exchanged a few words with Russell and then entered the school, a building of brick and wood and aluminum, representing a variety of construction projects over the years. My classroom was in the brick section, which was a little run-down but agreeable for its large windows and smell of fresh wax. The high ceiling was a maze of exposed pipes, twisting this way and that, like the ventricles of a massive brain that we had taken possession of.

"Don't be afraid, come on in," I told pupils in the hallway, who eyed me curiously, clutching their binders and book-bags. "Take a desk."

From the moment the bell rang, I didn't have time to be nervous. The morning went swiftly with Math and Earth Science, a nosebleed, and one incredibly shy little girl who refused to tell me her name. Her classmates revealed her secret, however—Ginny Rawlings—and her face reddened.

"You mean you didn't know?" she said hoarsely.

"Believe me," I told her. "There's a lot I don't know."

At lunch I escorted them to the cafeteria and then went to sit with my fellow teachers, most of whom I hadn't met. Our break was only thirty-five minutes and this fact weighed palpably on the conversations. Lunch was less a time for relaxation than a pit stop for refueling. Jaws worked in flex, and conversations came in bursts:

"Good summer?"

"Mmmm. You?"

"Worked on the house. New deck."

"Kit?"

"Mmmm. Gazebo, too."

"No way!"

I gulped with them and glanced up in time to see the minute hand of a large overhead clock jerk forward and then stop, trembling. Its broad, flat face was encased in a protective wire mesh because this space also served as the elementary school gymnasium. Basketball hoops hung at each end and on the backboards, in gleaming golden paint, appeared the unmistakable silhouettes of pigs.

"How was your morning?" asked Nelson, stirring his spoon in a cup. He was a large man who drank only coffee for lunch and taught art. We'd met a few days earlier when I'd been issued my keys.

"Fine," I said.

"I remember my first day on the job. I was scraping clay off the ceiling. Mrs. Heffernan's kids aren't giving you too much trouble, are they?"

"No, they're all right."

Mrs. Heffernan was my predecessor who, I'd been informed, had died over the summer. Her desk had been emptied before my arrival and the contents were put in several cartons beside it, with her name scrawled in magic marker. This morning I'd noticed pupils staring at the cartons, and I wondered how to get this stuff out of sight.

"You have any trouble, you just let me know," said a grey lady in a sleeveless dress, leaning into the conversation. Her naked arms were freckled and muscular, her face broad and tan.

I thanked her, pretending to remember who she was. We'd been introduced the same day I'd met Nelson, but her name hadn't sunk in. Now I felt her gaze on me, sizing me up.

"Most of your kids were in my class last year," she said. "They're not a bad bunch. You should do fine. If you keep them interested, discipline will take care of itself. That's the secret."

"I flap my arms and fly around the room," Nelson said. "That always works."

A young woman carried a tray to our table and sat down. She nodded in greeting to the group while shaking out her paper napkin. She paused at me.

"You're the new one," she said. "You're Stanley Mercer."

"That's right, and you're—"

"Shana. I was new here last year."

As she spoke she tore a roll in half, eating with her pink fingers. She started carefully, politely enough—but soon began to wolf it. I asked her what she taught.

"Special education," she said.

"Oh, then you must know Jimbo."

"His name is James," she corrected me, swallowing. "James Snow. The other children call him Jimbo, and he doesn't like it."

I almost told her about my bus ride, but then decided not to. It wouldn't sound right. She explained that Christine struggled less than James, who was more timid, too. Their mother was bringing up the kids by herself, and she had her hands full.

"Your job sounds tough, but it must be rewarding," I said.

"People like to say that." She shrugged, jabbing with her fork. "Mainly, a person has to learn to set up the good parts. That's what I've figured out, so far."

The table rattled; Nelson lumbered off, twisting his neck to the side, and it gave an audible *pop*.

"The problem is," she added as the bell rang, "the other kids still think mine are monsters."

I taught reading that afternoon and it was hot. Opening the windows made little difference, for this end-of-summer season offered no breeze. Some kids fidgeted, others rubbed their eyes, sleepy. Minutes crawled and I had to change the seating arrangement because a boy named Ty Carson was pestering Ester Xicay, a dark little bucktoothed girl who brought up the end of my class list. Ty made furtive blue ink marks on the back of Ester's neck. So I moved him to the front where I could keep an eye on him and for the rest of the afternoon he entertained himself by picking at a scab on his palm till it bled and left a spot on the front of his shirt, which I pretended not to see. Finally the day ended and he and the rest of my class escaped, and I erased the blackboard with a sense of relief.

Before locking up, I decided to move the cartons beside my desk marked *Mrs. Heffernan* to a less conspicuous place. A corner by the radiator would serve just fine. The first carton I carried over, but for the remaining two cartons I got lazy and starting pushing at them with my foot, sliding them across the floor. I wasn't paying much attention until the top carton toppled to the side with a crash.

"Damn!"

I didn't like the sound of the impact. Too many rattles. I was bending over to inspect the damage when a voice said to me, *"Hellooo. A little accident here?"*

It was the grey lady with freckled arms, striding toward me. Without missing a beat I picked up the carton and carried it to the radiator, set it down gently, and then returned to retrieve the last carton, which I put on top of the pile. "Yeah. Just trying to get some of this stuff out of the way and it tipped over."

She launched into a conversation, welcoming me and thrusting a baking tin into my hands. Her name was Patricia Gordon, she said. ("You didn't seem to remember me at lunch today. Call me Patty.") She'd taught here twenty-eight years. She was sure I'd like it. "And *those*," she said, "are my chocolate walnut squares."

She smelled of lilacs, and there was no doubting her friendly intentions, although she addressed me in the animated tones of the classroom. She was still switched ON. She announced that if I ever needed anything I should get in touch with her or her husband Roger. He knew everyone in the district, had served on the school board. He could take me pheasant hunting. Squeezing my arm, she asked me questions.

"What made you come to Legion?"

I tried to think of a good answer. A good lie.

"It's a prime place," I said. "Quality of life is what it comes down to, don't you think? I've always wanted to live in the country."

"Are you married?"

She looked at me with unblinking eyes. Suddenly I suspected that she saw right through me.

"No," I said. "I live alone."

I excused myself before she asked a question that I would regret answering. Outside, the other buses had left, but my fellow riders were still waiting. The smaller children ran around on the grass in frenetic circles, as if crazed, going nowhere. A boy explained to me that Russell was usually late because he worked at The Sportsman's Corner until three-thirty. I sat on the steps in the shade, where I could feel the cool concrete through the seat of my pants. Christine and James came out and sat down, close to me. They had doughy faces and oily skin; I realized it would take a while to get used to them. James still clutched his pencil, and he playfully tapped one of Christine's soft peach knees. I heard her say, "Scratch my back, Jim, I can't reach it."

He leaned over and raked her back with his fingers.

I slid closer to them.

"Hello Christine, Jim. Would you like a chocolate walnut square?"

Christine seemed pleased; she took one and thanked me. She nudged her brother. "Take one," she said. So he did. We chewed them and I began a conversation, *"Well Jim,"* which was interrupted when the bus pulled up and the doors popped open.

The smaller children scrambled and we followed them in step. I noticed that Jim had a piece of chocolate in the corner of his mouth, clinging to the edge of his lips, like a fat black fly. It bothered me. It was conspicuous, and I wanted him to wipe the spot off before the other children saw it. *Been eatin' shit again?* I could hear them say. I stared at the chocolate and was tempted to reach out and flick it away. He saw me looking at him. When I averted my eyes, he suddenly spoke.

"Why do you call me Jim?"

There was suspicion in his voice.

"Isn't that your name?"

He began to speak and then stopped; began again and stopped. His hesitation was not as if he couldn't find his words; rather, it seemed the words were too great to get out. His throat convulsed and a tiny trace of saliva slipped to his lips, hanging there for an excruciating second, until he wiped it off with the back of his hand. The chocolate went with it. He turned and boarded the bus. Christine thrust herself between us, quite boldly, using her bulk in a protective manner. She climbed the steps and left me with the sight of her broad hips and pale blonde head. I followed and went past Russell, who now wore sunglasses and a baseball cap. He tipped his cap to me, which I found vaguely distressing. I nodded to him.

The riders were subdued until we went down the rutted lane. Then, as if on cue, all attention was focused on Jim and Christine. A chorus of *"Bye Bye Jimbo"* and *"Bye Darling Christine!"* filled the bus, along with an accompaniment of smooching sounds. They got off and the doors closed with a smack. The bus backed away from the house, and suddenly, a new cry went up. Children began to lean out of windows and point. We were passing a garden and a line of rabbit cages that bordered the lane. *"There he is! It's Billy! There he is!"* I saw a blond child in cut-off denim shorts. He had been hiding behind the rabbit cages. Now he panicked at the voices, he raced through the garden rows and tripped, kicking up a spray of dirt clods. His chin skidded on the ground. He pulled himself out of the tangle, assaulted by the school bus bedlam of *"Billy! Billy!"* and went crashing into the stalks of corn, and disappeared.

"My God," I said. "Who was that?"

"That's Billy Snow," said a boy. He seemed overjoyed. "He's the one who doesn't talk or go to school. They say he twists off the heads of rabbits and it's true. It's true!"

The bus dropped me off at my farmhouse. Russell backed out of the driveway, and before going to my door, I reached inside my mailbox, my hand stirring the air.

No letters today.

🍂

Some nights after school I took a portable grill and charcoal bricks to the river's edge and broiled a pork chop and drank beer. I listened to a Chicago ball game on a radio, slapped mosquitoes. Later I threw the burnt charcoal into the river and watched it steam and hiss.

I had plenty of time to think. I'd spent the first part of my childhood in a small town which was not so very different from Legion, a place with a central square of flat-roofed buildings and a grain elevator and starlings that perched on telephone poles, scolding you when you walked by. They left pasty droppings on parking meters.

But I'd been out of the country—and I don't mean these cornfields and silos, I mean E Pluribus, the United States—for fourteen years. Pursuing a childhood dream.

While my family moved to the suburbs and everybody else of my generation was getting mortgages and having kids and settling down, I'd been trying to improve my throwing arm. Experimenting with my batting stance. Adapting to injuries. I was a baseball player. That might sound like an unlikely career to pursue abroad but it was true. I started out in the U.S., but discovered that dreams don't respect borders.

After a sports scholarship in college I was picked in the pro draft, and moved quickly from Class A to Eastern League to AAA in Indianapolis. This was a time of great hope, of hovering possibility, a time when anything good that happened seemed like my due. Stanley Mercer was going places—*naturally!* I was slow to see other forces, and utterly unprepared when injuries pushed me back and my career stalled, when people began to doubt my future. But I stayed true to my dream, because I knew that I must be right, even if it involved certain adjustments along the way, delays in my ultimate success. I accepted my first foreign contract in a Mexican league, and kept working and practicing. This was followed by winter ball in Las Macias, Dominican Republic, and then in a now-defunct European league.

I ended my playing days barnstorming and playing exhibitions for the Paris Buffaloes. A life devoted to my dream, never giving up—nobody ever accused this Stanley of not hustling—and now, in the fading summer, this is where I found myself: Legion, Iowa.

Standing by the muddy river, I smelled the last bloom of prairie summer in the air, and I still couldn't quite believe it.

❧

ONLY A month earlier I'd been beside a pumping ocean with wind off the cliffs. My girlfriend Delphine and I had joined my boss, Monsieur Chedin, and his family at their vacation home in Tauzé-le-Mignon.

At that time I was still trying to ingratiate myself and save my job. My plan was to persuade my boss about the merits of playing baseball in the summer. It seemed obvious to me. But Monsieur Chedin was against the idea, because that was when the French went on holiday.

"But that's precisely the point," I told him, extracting an olive pit from my mouth and tossing it in a bush, "there'll be more people with the free time to come see us—we'd be a

– 19 –

leisure attraction. Soccer is dead in August. People get tired of the beach. We could offer an alternative. That's when we should play our exhibitions. It's money waiting to be made."

Chedin scratched his chin, shook his head. He didn't want to hear about it because that was when he took his vacation, too. Every year he came down to this sun-soaked, orange stone village where he sat for a month under a parasol and drank a syrupy sweet booze fabricated by monks at the nearby monastery and watched his children listlessly scuff their toes in the dust, which was no doubt made up of centuries of bones of earlier monks. The children scratched their mosquito bites and complained of boredom. There was no beach in this town, only cliffs; you could hear the sea crash and roar, gulls spurted up over the edge like the white of spray, but, if you drew nearer, looked down, you saw the water far below, churning.

"Nothing gets dated faster than the latest idea," he said.

"You're not even giving it a chance!"

I couldn't hide my desperation. He hadn't spoken of renewing my contract. Delphine, whose father owned a chain of sporting goods stores and was one of the few remaining sponsors of the Paris Buffaloes, tried to help me:

"If you did something in August, you could tie it in with some of the music festivals, don't you think?" she put in. "Be part of something bigger."

Chedin removed his hat, adjusted its band. (He'd confided in me that his head was very particular and it was almost impossible to find his size.) Then, with a smile, he suggested to Delphine that she take his kids swimming. The drive was only eight kilometers down the road. "That would be very constructive of you," he told her. He turned to me, lifted the bottle, asked: "Some more?"

Delphine pushed back her chair, snatched up her sunglasses. "Let's go, Stanley."

"What's the matter?" I asked.

"Are you blind? I've had enough!"

She stalked off.

Chedin took another sip and shrugged. I hesitated to follow (after all, he was my boss) and I think it was *that* hesitation, only a matter of seconds, which marked a point of no return. Delphine and I had lived together for almost four years. I'm not saying that moment decided everything, of course not—relationships die by steps, not by thunderbolts—but if I hadn't hesitated, it is possible that the day would've finished differently. Perhaps something would've remained retrievable, and I would still be on the other side of the water, trying to make things work. But at that moment I was worried about the wrong thing, obsessing even, and this made me slow to react responsibly. This was how things went over the brink.

I hurried after her. My delay, I repeat, was only a matter of seconds. But by then Delphine had reached her car, an old blue 2CV that roared to life and whisked out of a nearby hangar. As she bore down on me, Delphine didn't slow down, she was taking no passengers, and for reasons of self-preservation I jumped out of the way. Without a pause the car skidded into the street, headed toward the square with a characteristic Citroën wheeze. I listened for the change of gears, and then listened till I could hear no more.

What now? How long before she came back? I wondered. The sun's rays and the angles of rooftops throbbed, hurting my eyes. God, this drink was strong! Rather than return to Chedin I went over to the shade of a spindly linden tree where I sat down, mulling it over. What to do? Then I let my eyes close for just a minute—

When I awoke suddenly and lifted my head, squinted toward the terrasse, Delphine was nowhere in sight but my boss was still sitting under the parasol. From the monastery chapel came the sound of a bell, *Ping-doinng, Ping-doinng,* almost frantic. I recall a violent sensation of being dislocated, stronger than any I'd ever known. I blinked and sat up and brushed twigs off my elbow, like a man who'd fallen out of the sky. *Ping-doinng, Ping-doinng.* My mouth opened and a low cry escaped. I believed it utterly impossible to return to my old assumptions.

☙

M<small>Y BROTHER</small> Riley takes credit for my getting a job in Legion, but I can't blame him for what I did later, for the trouble that inspired this book. Riley has done well in life. He works as an attorney in Evanston, his ties match his socks, and he sends my mother expensive cheeses for Christmas. (He's sensitive about jokes at the expense of lawyers and considers them a new form of bigotry.) When we were kids he used to shoot at my feet with a BB gun and say *"Dance!"* It was something he'd seen on television. I danced. I thought everything he did was great and wanted to be like him.

When I left college and NCAA baseball, he sent me a gift check with a note which had been scrawled in knuckly letters on his law firm's watermark stationery. It said:

> DON'T FUCK UP.
> LOVE,
> RILEY

That's good advice, but it's hard to follow. Years later, after Delphine dumped me and Chedin fired me, I showed up jet-lagged and exhausted at Riley's doorstep in the suburbs of Chicago, still carrying my kit bag with cleats and glove (reaching for the doorbell with the strap digging into my shoulder, I thought: how ridiculous for a man my age!). Soon I found myself sitting on a sofa, eating a piece of cake off a plate, flipping through an album of photographs of his little boys, while these same little boys raced and screamed around the room, and one of them, Justin, came forward and kicked me on the shin.

"Ow!" I exclaimed.

"Speck, it's great to see you!" Riley said as I rubbed my bone, waiting for him to scold the boy, but all he said was: "He

– 22 –

just wants to prove you're real. Hey, Serena, did you expect we'd see old Speck?"

(This was a family nickname; my brother never called me Stanley.)

"Well—" she looked at me with something less than enthusiasm, "no."

"You're looking good," Riley told me. "Still in shape, I see."

"Yeah—nice place you got here," I replied. Riley must've let out his belt four notches and he was losing his hair, but this house was unquestionably first-rate. The carpet, upholstery and walls were an ivory plush; in my fatigued state, I felt as if I were falling into cotton. When I asked to use the bathroom, he gave me directions to several. Whereas everything I owned, and I mean down to the last pair of sneakers and the $276 stuffed in my shaving pouch, fit into the lumpy duffle beside the coffee table. "Say, do you remember that note you wrote me when I got out of school?" I asked him.

No, he said, he didn't. (Though maybe this was just a kindness.) But he was very understanding about letting me stay. At the beginning it was like a reunion—Riley and I went out and got drunk three nights in a row; he listened to my tale and told me I would rebound, I would come back: you couldn't keep a good man down. ("Yeah, but what about me?") He was a patient, loyal brother. *You're a Mercer, you got the gift of gab! Never underestimate that!*

Still, it was obvious that this situation couldn't last. I had to take measures. There's a limit to waking up in someone else's house and sneaking the toothpaste and oh-so-carefully sponging out the sink so as not to leave a single hair; there's only so much pleasant conversation to make about the children, those little geniuses. I offered to cut the grass, just to make myself useful, but Riley wouldn't let me; he relied on a "lawn management specialist" who came in and did it for him. Worst of all, his wife Serena started giving me The Stare. I saw her at the window, or across the table: an unmistakable gaze reserved only for me. Serena was unstintingly polite and didn't say anything disagreeable, but she had a way of not saying anything that was so chilly you could feel it from afar. Like a breeze off an iceberg. Before, I'd been the far-off brother in uniform, exotic. Now I was just plain Bad News.

A job was a must. I'd majored in journalism in college and had almost finished a degree but had never worked in the profession. From the beginning, I'd concentrated all my energies on trying to *play*. But no one outside of sports could take you seriously for that approach. Newspapers were downsizing aggressively; broadcasting had never heard of me. There was no market for my kind of experience. I was out of step.

INTERVIEWER (*gazing intently at me over his glasses*): Our human resources profile includes self-assessment. What would you say is your greatest fault?

ME (*returning his gaze, strangled by the tie I borrowed from Riley, conscious of coffee gurgling in my stomach*): Well—I work too hard.

And that might've gotten me the job, if I hadn't started laughing. Honestly, I wasn't a lazy person, I wasn't afraid to hustle. But the American business world took me by surprise. It wasn't only hard-nosed, which I could deal with, something I expected. It was also—and this was the paradoxical and shocking part—*sentimental*. Potential employers seemed to want something more than my willingness to trade my time and do their bidding: they demanded something intangible, signs of my belief in their enterprise, my devotion. My God, they were needy!

My interview at a convenience store that was robbed twice a week went very well, though, and the next morning, as I was pondering whether to take the job (I could start next Saturday, provided the results of my drug test were negative), I telephoned my mother to ask if I might stay at her place for a brief period, just to take some of the pressure off Riley and Serena.

I was feeling very low, to tell the truth; my morale had hit bottom. So far, in front of my family, I'd made an effort to keep up appearances and, when necessary, lied, because I knew that they couldn't solve my problems. When you're no longer a kid, you realize that you have to play the game, any game, with pain. But now I was beginning to despair. At first I'd been distracted by the changed surroundings and dealing with jet lag; but, within a week, a powerful ache overwhelmed me, a sort of *regret* lag, which infected my every thought and gesture, and reduced me to bitterness. So much failure, so much effort: for nothing. When Riley asked in a helpful tone, "What do you *really* want to do, Speck?" I felt that I could walk around the house and start kicking out the windows. Of course I didn't. But that was how I felt. Above all, I was aware that a new season had begun and I wasn't ready and there was no one to blame but myself. No longer was it a matter of *playing* at home. Playing? And where was home?

"Listen, Mom," I said over the telephone, "do you think I could move in with you for a short time, while I'm sorting things out?"

There was a pause on her end of the line. The pause lengthened. And lengthened some more. It was mortifying.

"Well, uh, of course you're welcome here, Stanley. You know that. It's just a matter of timing, see. Could you hold off a few days? Archie's back in town."

Archie was her new boyfriend, a traveling salesman of frozen juice concentrate. My father was long dead, and my mother's love life, after my long absence, was something of a revelation to me. When I'd stopped by her place earlier in the week to rummage through her hall closet in search of my childhood baseball card collection, which I hoped to sell off for quick cash, I'd noticed a man's jacket. It caught my eye because of its striking color, an electric cranberry. I felt like calling: "Hey Mom, this guy you're seeing, is he gay?" But I held my tongue. Why say something stupid when she was clearly happy? My mother had greeted me at the door wearing a silk blouse and black skirt cinched by a large leather belt. Her grey hair was clipped stylishly short. Her appearance was a statement. A statement of sex, basically. A little unnerving, but who was I to argue? Now I told her:

"Hey, it was just a thought. I'll come visit some other time. No problem."

Gently replacing the phone on the wall, I turned back to the kitchen table.

"I'm cramping her style. Maybe I'll go to a motel for a little while."

Riley was buttering a bagel, dressed for work in his jacket; his face looked puffy. "No. You couldn't do that, Speck." He thought about it for three seconds. "Could you?"

Then Serena came to the rescue. She folded down the newspaper and said, "How about this, guys? *'Tri-State agency seeks teachers—temporary certification available to anyone with a B.A., B.S. or equivalent. Substitute positions, flexible contracts.'*"

 ❦

IT WAS only a small lie, claiming on the forms that I'd finished my college degree. I was only a few credits short. For a fee, the agency would clear my paperwork with the state. I had no illusions about the job that awaited me, either. If the scheme succeeded, I expected to end up in some inner-city school. Not much safer than a convenience store, perhaps, but at least offering a day shift and insurance benefits. It would get me on my feet. It would involve real responsibilities, too, nothing to sneer at. But then came the curve ball:

Legion, Iowa?

The town was a blue dot on the map.

I borrowed money from my brother, bought a used car from a dealer called Big Dale, and invested in several white shirts.

I said my goodbyes and followed the signs to the entrance ramp of the Eisenhower Expressway and slipped into the flow of outbound traffic. Cars and lanes peeled off but I kept rolling west, and eventually Chicago and suburbs were behind me, and I was zooming across open country.

My car started heating up shortly before I crossed the Mississippi, but I wasn't too concerned, not at first. I let the engine cool at a rest stop while I studied the map, wishing I had the time to follow the river, fantasizing a trip, imagining what I might see along the way. It was tempting: why not travel down that fundamental fold in America? But no, that wasn't serious; I owed people money and I had a respectable job awaiting me. So I contented myself with choosing back roads for the rest of my trip to Legion, a route that took me through towns like Muscatine, Wellman and What Cheer, then Oskaloosa and Promise City and Gravity.

"Delphine," I said into the air, wondering what she was doing now, "who can resist Gravity?"

By the time my car limped into Legion, I was cursing Big Dale. The panel lights blinked nonsensically and the engine had started to make a peculiar rattle and I felt lucky to have made it this far. I stopped under the shade of a big pin oak tree and opened the hood and felt the heat radiate against my face. *What now?* My shirt was soaked with sweat. Nearby, a short man with a copper complexion was brushing white paint onto the side of a clapboard church; he paused to look at me. He dipped his brush, slapped some on, and then turned to look at me again. This made me uneasy, so I left my car with the hood up and went for a walk.

My first look at Legion did not impress me. Aside from a convenience store called Jaycee's that I'd passed on the main road, there was a town square consisting of a scruffy park with a basketball hoop, a concrete water fountain that didn't work, and benches where some old men sat and spat at the squirrels. Block-lettered signs announced that I had entered a tobacco-free zone. A brownstone bank occupied one corner of the square, and businesses included Leroy's Supermarket, a diner called Dwight's (*ALL-U-CAN EAT CATFISH FRIDAY*), a video rental outlet attached to a Christian bookstore, and a junky consignment shop called Tomorrow's Treasures.

The nearby houses were neat and well-maintained, but seemed to cling close to the earth as if flattened by too much exposure to the sky. There were plenty of American flags on porches or in front windows. Several blocks from the town square, I came upon the building which served as the elementary and middle school. Since today was Saturday, it was closed and quiet. I leaned against a piece of playground equipment and, while I tried to collect my thoughts, a dog trotted across the grass and paused to piss on the bricks. It looked me directly in the eye, and then shambled off.

So: this was where I'd landed. Pressing my fingers to my temples, in my mind I heard an echo, *Ping-doinng, Ping-doinng.*

❦

MRS. GORDON saved me those first few weeks. It was a nervous time, so much so that I slept badly at night and my digestion seemed out of whack. Luckily for me, she offered to let me observe her class during the pauses when mine was otherwise occupied with music or a recess. This opportunity to learn kept me out of serious trouble—frankly, I aped her, for it was a crazy idea to put a person with zero experience in charge of a classroom. The earliest days I got by with a lot of pretending, in the manner a person who's been drinking feigns sobriety or an actor puts on an Italian accent; I let it be known that I was Mr. Teacher, and thereafter tried not to stumble all over the place, or otherwise fall out of character.

Since most of my pupils had had Mrs. Gordon as a teacher the previous year, when I imitated one of her methods, they acted on the cue. Other pupils, seeing them act, generally followed. This didn't always work, but when it did my life was less stressful and I went through a period where it seemed

I did everything like Mrs. Gordon short of working in drag. Although teaching was new to me, I'd always had a strong competitive streak, and tried to treat this situation as another test. I'd show them—and I'd show me, too.

Mrs. Gordon gave me an earful, though. How she could talk! She craved an audience, and it was no small commitment, being her listener. In the process I learned plenty of gossip about my colleagues. Nelson the art teacher, she confided, was divorced and on a diet. He really wanted to be principal, a position occupied by a hairless man named Worthington, who used to be a music teacher until he could take it no longer. Mr. Worthington was unhappy with Shana Linn, the special education teacher, because she didn't want to help out with Bernie Week. "She's a bit of a snob, she wears sunglasses like she thinks she's famous or something. We're counting on you to help out, too."

"Bernie Week?" I asked.

"Yes, you know, at homecoming. The whole week before the football game there are various Bernie activities."

"Bernie activities?"

"Sure. You've seen Bernie. You know, the pig."

It was true that I'd noticed pig caricatures in many places at the school. Not only in the cafeteria, but painted on an equipment shed, for instance, and on kids' T-shirts. The local mascot, I'd assumed. But I hadn't known his name.

"Why's he called Bernie?"

"It's short for the tan Bernington, the kind of hog they say was popular in this part of the state in the nineteenth century. Sandy body, white socks. Now he's mainly disappeared and you see other breeds, the market has changed, but people still respect the history. Some people might think that it's silly or a backward thing, to name ourselves after a hog. But that's partly the point. You think we don't know how other people feel about pigs? That attitude doesn't impress anybody around here. We know the score, they don't. Why apologize for a Bernie? What's wrong with a pig, anyway? For generations people have made their living hog farming and this town—this school—depends on it, too, and that's nothing to be ashamed of. You see what I'm saying?"

"Sure, sure."

"So now you're a Bernie, too. You didn't even know it!"

❦

My final discovery about Legion, though, was closer to home. And more perturbing. My farmhouse, I learned, had a criminal reputation.

"That's where you live?" people said. *"Hmmm."*

Apparently, it was common knowledge locally that a few months before my arrival, the place had been the site of a major methamphetamine bust. The previous renters had been charged with manufacturing the stuff on the premises. There'd also been a shooting, though fortunately the victim had survived. On the kitchen wall you could see acne-like marks. These, I realized after moving in, were embedded shotgun pellets. It wasn't obvious at first, or at least I'd been temporarily blind to the fact. I'd expected the peaceful country life. Not drug dealers settling scores.

None of this history had been mentioned to me by my landlord, a farmer named Mr. Simms who wore an old chambray shirt and a dirty feed cap but who, people informed me, was one of the largest landowners in the area. He'd pointed out the shining new kitchen sink and bathtub, which made a favorable impression in an otherwise run-down setting. Mr. Simms had said, "I'll give you a good price because I don't want to leave the house empty. That attracts trouble, you know."

Behind the house was a large backyard and leaning sheds surrounded by raspberry bushes; wasps buzzed in and out of mud nests under the overhangs. Barely a week after my conversation with Mr. Simms, I found an old denim jacket hanging on a nail in one of these sheds with a wad of twenty-dollar bills in one pocket: I counted out thirty-two of them, $640 in all. You couldn't even say that the money was hidden, but somehow the police had missed it when they scoured the place after the bust. For safekeeping, I slipped the money into my pocket.

Beyond the sheds was an overgrown orchard where an old wooden wagon and beehive supers rotted in the weeds. These were traces of an earlier way of life. On a corner pole, mounted high enough to see from my upstairs bedroom window, was a bell. One evening I walked along the fence and went over to the bell and pulled its rusty chain, as farmwives must've done in bygone days to call in their men from the field.

But the bell didn't ring. There was no sound, just a feeble squeak of its mounting. Looking up, I saw that the bell had no clapper.

☾

Sunset. I went inside the house and began to do push-ups and sit-ups in front of the television, exercising more out of nervousness than for any kind of training. One program showed a guy and a girl doing exercises, too. Lars and Sapphire. They wore slinky tights and kept complimenting each other on their buns. Change the channel, thirty more leg lifts.

Never had television seemed so otherworldly to me. Everyone on the screen looked rich and upset. It was an America in which Legion did not exist, a world where only the losers were ugly—there was never much doubt about who was a winner and who was a loser. And, if there was a depiction of a school, it was in one of those movies that come out every couple of years (the clothes change but they're always the same), films that pretend to be gritty and hip, where teachers are rebels, too, and you never saw kids like Jim or Christine Snow.

In Legion, truth be told, we didn't have a cool soundtrack. No one saw a diary of our days. That night the television annoyed me so much that I wanted to unplug it and carry it down to the river and throw it into a scum-bank. I could watch it sink. This would be appropriate and entertaining at the same time.

"*Can you manage the skill sets to impact the knowledge economy*—"

I turned off the program and stepped outside, cooling my bare feet in the dew, and began to urinate in my backyard. While I peed I looked up at the sky and the stars which salted its surface. In the distance of the darkened river, bullfrogs groinked. The real game was only just beginning. The consequences of choices. I zipped up my pants and wondered what I would tell my pupils tomorrow.

2

"*Onward, Bernie, forward, Bernie, fight on for your fame!*"

Mine was a peculiar job; in addition to explaining the solar eclipse by displaying light bulbs and revolving one dramatically around my head, I was supposed to be a certain kind of person. A Bernie kind of person. Someone who could strap on a flesh-colored, rubber pig nose and in moments of pressure stomp my feet and squeal: at Legion sporting events, this was our special community cheer, the soul behind the school song. Hundreds of people lifting their noses skyward, shrilling in unison, creating a Legion yell whose reputation had spread throughout the state. This earsplitting ritual was famous for unnerving opponents, leading to fumbles and blown free throws.

I might've suspected that Legion loyalists would oink, but Mrs. Gordon patiently explained to me that *oinking* was what you found in cartoons and story clichés of the uninformed, whereas a pig in fact had a considerable repertoire of sounds and the "oink" figured among the least important. It hardly rated above a snuffle. The squeal, however, was the unmistakable signature. A cry from the heart.

The Legion pep club gave me a rubber nose but I hadn't got round to using it yet. Other teachers played along with the custom, wore their noses on football Friday nights and to rallies, but I was reluctant. (Baseball fans, I flattered myself to think, were less inclined to such displays.) My own little snout remained undisturbed in a dresser drawer, where I fully intended it to stay. I admit, though, that when I brought it home that first day I tried it on for several seconds in front of my bathroom mirror. (When you're given something like that, who can resist trying, just once?) Seemed innocuous, except when I breathed hard. Then the nose made a rasping sound and wrinkled a little, and suddenly I looked both dumb and evil. My eyes seemed smaller, too. They say a pig is actually rather smart and social, so maybe it was just me.

"Take the ball right down the field"

As the light bulb went round my head, I warned my class, "Remember, you should never look at the sun directly. It will burn your eyes out." My pupils shuddered in delight and shielded their faces with spidery hands. They liked fearsome threats.

Then I gave the standard crushing talk about the vastness of the universe, how our sun was only one of millions of suns in our galaxy and these suns were millions of miles apart, and our galaxy—imagine!—was one of millions of galaxies. Tens, even hundreds of millions!

"It's all right to scream," I said. "Just this once."

Some hesitated, considering.

But most of them barely blinked. The world down here was sufficient, thank you very much.

Now a pupil called out, "Do you know why old people get wrinkled?"

I called back, "Raise your hand first."

He raised his hand and repeated the question. The boy's name was Brian Rush. He thought he was smart and he liked to sign his papers "Brain Rush." At first I believed that he was trying to be a pet, so I didn't call on him too often, but then it became clear that he didn't mind irritating me. He definitely wasn't trying to be a pet.

"They get wrinkled," I replied, "as a symptom of age."

"But why is it that symptom and not some other symptom?"

"There are lots of symptoms. White hair. Stiff joints. A general slowing down. There are lots—"

"Sure there are lots," he interrupted. "But why *that* one?"

In truth I couldn't explain why old people got wrinkled. I didn't have a clue. It was one of the millions of things—hundreds of millions—that I didn't know, but I wasn't going to admit it to Brain Rush in front of the class. "Listen, it's nature's way," I said, turning toward the blackboard, preparing to change the subject, only to hear him announce, "*I know.*"

I faced him again. "Good for you, Brian. And I suppose you're going to tell us?"

"It's the belly button," he said, "where all a person's skin comes together? When you get older, your belly button starts coming loose."

A few pupils laughed but he wasn't trying to be funny or cute (one look at his smug toadish face made it clear to anybody that this kid was post-cute); most of the class grew silent, thinking it over. His words probably sounded as reasonable as anything I'd told them today.

What was really being learned? Who was fooling whom? Earlier that same morning, my brother Riley had telephoned, in answer to a message I'd left on his service, asking if I could stop by his place on a future weekend if I came through Chicago on "business." (The truth was, there was a woman I'd met in a bar shortly before taking the job in Legion, and I wanted to visit her. After a few weeks by myself in the country, I was hankering for more than Friday night football.) The timing of Riley's return call was bad; I was running late, and had just noticed that a shaving cut had left a large blood-spot on my white shirt collar. It was my last clean shirt, so I was standing in front of the mirror with a bottle of Liquid Ghost, a correcting fluid intended for use on office paper, trying to apply a drop to the stain. Then the phone rang.

"Speck!" he said, "How's tricks?"

"Not bad. The usual. Hey, could I call you back tonight?"

"Sure, sure. I just wanted to let you know that I got your message and we'd be glad to see you. I'm wondering how you like it out there. Did I ever tell you about the time I was passing by our old neighborhood, the park where you played so much ball, and I thought, What the hey, I'll check it out—"

"Listen, Riley, I got to go to work. Could—"

"When I got there, I was walking along the grass under some trees, when all of a sudden, *whamp!* I tripped and fell flat on my face. There I was, sprawled under the maples. Hurt like hell! When I looked back to see what I'd tripped over, it wasn't a root or something. You know what I saw?"

"What?"

"It was a slide. Remember the one we played on when we were kids? I mean, now it seemed *so small!*"

I hesitated. Snorts of laughter came through my receiver.

"Oh," I said. "Quite the joke, Riley."

"Still the same old Speck! I had you going, didn't I? Ever the eager beaver, cut out to be a believer! You never give up, do you? Better watch yourself, dude."

"Later, okay?"

This conversation annoyed me, but that morning as I stood in front of the class and looked at Brain Rush and all the other little heads, I wondered if Riley had a point. I experienced the strange sensation that I'd been here twenty-five years ago, in this very room, only my desk was pine instead of plastic. And over there, in the corner, was a boy who might be me. The Kincaid kid. He wore thick foggy glasses. I could imagine him in the grandstand, mouthing the words:

Score a touchdown every time!

Anita, a cinnamon guinea pig, lived in a cage in the back of the classroom. She was a hot-blooded little creature who ate alfalfa pellets all day and then shat them out again. Ginny Rawlings had brought her to school, asking in her small gravel voice, "She'll be okay here, won't she? My mom says she'll be." I wavered for a moment, and then relented. (Thinking:

thanks a bunch, Mom! What else can I do for you?) As it happened, Anita was an instant success, as popular as computer games in the library, and certainly more practical than a true-to-life Bernie. I had to make a waiting list for pig privileges at recess.

One day, two boys got in a fight—one had been absent and missed his pig turn, and now tried to claim it—and Anita was in between, the center of a tug of war. She squealed so loudly that I imagined her stretching, pig toffee, till she got away when I grabbed the boys and shook them. Anita hurtled through the air, a fur missile and, as I bent into the fracas, I accidentally took an elbow to the eye.

"Shit!"

The boys stopped and looked at me. Their teacher had just said something that no one was supposed to say, and instantly all the children in the classroom reacted, the noise level went straight up. I felt around my eye, blinking, and then—oh, for God's sake—my contact lens slipped out. I looked at my fingers. Where did it go? I touched my cheek, up and down. Damn! I got down on my hands and knees.

"Quiet down now! Nobody move!"

My voice resounded, bouncing off walls. I didn't like to yell, but it's tricky to maintain authority while crawling. My eye stung and its lid fluttered as I peered in all directions, feeling around the floor when, suddenly, I felt another presence, a sensation of being observed. I looked around. There, in the doorway, stood Mr. Worthington.

Without a word he backed into the hallway.

And then I turned away from his empty space, from the cawing children, and I saw Anita peeking at me from under the radiator. She bucked her head, as if challenging me.

Onward, Bernie, forward Bernie . . .

By lunchtime, when I retreated to the cafeteria, my eye was puffed and blueish. I hadn't found the lens, so I had to rely on the contact lens in the other eye. The imbalance was a strain but there was no choice but to put up with it.

I walked past a table where Jim and Christine ate alone ("Hey," I said, and they stared silently), past the other children who sucked on straws, to the far side where Nelson and Mrs. Gordon conversed. I lowered my tray and sat down, avoiding direct eye contact.

"My goodness," said Mrs. Gordon. "What happened to you?"

"The bastards got him," said Nelson.

"Just a little accident," I said, assuming we could talk of something else. But they wanted to hear the story, so I told them, while they shook their heads. Mrs. Gordon offered to stop by and say a few words to my class to restore discipline, a suggestion which I immediately refused, for any scoldings should come from me. Nelson said my eye looked like a piss hole in the snow. That's about how it felt, too. Tingly, hot and cool.

"Something wrong with the other eye too?" he asked.

He'd noticed my squint. The lone lens was getting to me; I needed a patch like a pirate. A headache had begun to spread, a throbbing weblike sensation across the front of my skull. Now he laughed and pointed to my lunch tray. "How about applying that raw slab to your shiner? It's too deadly to eat."

"Don't start on him," said Mrs. Gordon.

I looked down at my pork patty. "Huh?"

"Trichinosis," he said. "Haven't you heard of trichinosis? These cafeteria cooks don't give a damn, they cook pork in a hurry and feed it to the kids. It's scandalous. I read an article about it. You can die from eating uncooked pork. Tiny worms rape your insides."

He lifted his coffee cup and emptied it with one toss. I could feel the liquid burning down his throat.

"If you ask me," said Mrs. Gordon, "he just doesn't want anyone else to eat, since he's not eating."

The entire conversation struck me as hallucinatory. Everything I ate here was overcooked. And, anyway, lately I'd been fighting some unpleasant strain in my guts, so this bland school regime didn't bother me. Now I picked up the mustard container and coaxed out a few splurts. I looked around the cafeteria at the children and pondered the possibility of trichinae worms in their intestines, boring holes, going about their wormy business. A common bond.

"Gee, Stanley. What's the matter with your face?"

Shana Linn lowered her tray, and sat down with us. Over her shoulder I saw the encased clock on the wall, the minute hand jerked forward, trembling. I felt trapped and answered her vaguely, and then got up to leave. I didn't want anybody looking at me.

Rah! Rah! Rah!

Back in the classroom, my eye was a showpiece. At first I tried to conduct classes as usual, but my kids were distracted. They weren't really looking at me; they were looking at the eye. I explained long division, that one mustn't forget to bring down the zero, and they tittered.

I tossed away the chalk. Useless. Might as well lecture in a clown suit. I sat at my desk.

"Come here. Everybody gather round."

Now they were timid. But I insisted, and they drew near.

"The bruise you see is from smashed blood vessels. The blood seeps out into the deep layer of my skin. It looks blue because the blood is still far from the surface, and it'd be red if the skin were actually broken."

They crowded closer, a confluence of eyes and chins and nervous shuffling.

"The swelling is fluid that accumulates in spaces between the cells. It's like a sponge up there, sort of. Remember the cells you looked at under the microscope?"

Some of them frowned. I was taking the fun out of it. Then a familiar voice asked: "Can I touch it?"

A thrill went through the crowd, as palpable as a pulse, as Brain Rush stepped forward.

"Go easy, then," I told him.

Of course other kids had to touch it after him; each took a turn at the wound. It pleased them. Fortunately it was numb, not tender at all. With my good eye I could see Ginny Rawlings and Ester Xicay and a few others holding back, but still watching, while pressures of touch described my misshapen contours, my deformity. My imagination meandered and suddenly it wasn't me, it was Jim and Christine whom the children wanted to touch; they crowded closer and closer, hands outstretched—and I was in the crowd, too. I wanted to touch, and understand.

"You know one day I was peeling an apple," Brain Rush said breathlessly, "and I cut the ball of my thumb and blood seeped out, it wouldn't stop, it just kept bubbling out from the slit, and the throb got to my head and all of a sudden I could feel that I was full of the stuff, inside me, and there were purple organs swimming around in it, and my bones were floating. And I looked at the apple in my hand and for a second I thought that it was my heart, and it could start pumping and spurting—"

There was a crash, and now he was lying on the floor. A cry went up, and I told everyone to stand back and give him air. For God's sake! Many things went through my mind as I knelt beside him and massaged his wrists and looked at his ashen face and the twitch of his closed eyelids. Was he going to be okay? Should I call the school nurse? Wait, no—this school didn't have a school nurse. An ambulance? But I couldn't leave him, could I? Then he opened his eyes and, with my assistance, sat up, rubbing the back of his head.

"Are you okay?" I asked, hoping mightily that he was, for my sake, because his parents might be just as nutty as their son. If he was hurt, would they sue me?

"Yeah," he said dreamily and, for the rest of the afternoon, he sat quietly at his desk, fondly caressing the lump on his head.

☾

"So you're the guy who lives in the meth house."

I was buying a used Yamaha 650 motorcycle from a skinny man named Hutch who looked at me disapprovingly. The motorcycle interested me because it was cheap and because I wanted very much to get away to Chicago for the next weekend. Hutch had a tattoo on his arm and it said *"Suck Suck."* Even then, I realized that I'd always remember this conversation because of Hutch's tattoo. It was a squiggly blue effort whose repetition of the word was an inspired stroke—one *"Suck"* simply wouldn't have had the same badass magic.

"It's not a meth house anymore," I said.

He scowled and studied my face. It occurred to me that his unfriendly attitude might also have something to do with some cream I'd dabbed on my upper cheek and brow. I'd gone to the drugstore and bought a tube of the kind of stuff that kids use to cover their pimples, and applied it around my black eye. I looked better for work that way. But it was different in Hutch Suck Suck's backyard, beside his woodpile and chainsaw and burning trash barrel. I squared my shoulders and lifted my chin and stared back at him without blinking. Stanley Mercer might wear makeup but he could act like a tough motherfucker, too.

"We got to stay away from that tweaky shit," he said.

"I agree," I said. "Now do you want my money or not?"

This question got results. A minute later I was counting out twenties onto Hutch's palm.

Methamphetamine was a drug I knew very little about, partly because of a generational difference. My generation had done endless bongs, kids with money snorted coke, and almost everybody drank too much beer. Lots of ballplayers did speed

– 41 –

of a milder sort and, in my time in Europe, North African hashish and very strong homegrown weed were popular, socially. But meth didn't enter the picture. Maybe I was naive but I hadn't even *heard* of methamphetamine before coming to Iowa. Clearly it had made a stir around here. I looked at the pockmarks on my kitchen wall every morning as I munched my breakfast cereal, and I wondered.

People at school spoke of the relative simplicity of making meth, from cough formula and antifreeze and recycled lithium batteries, or stolen anhydrous ammonia intended for agricultural purposes. It was a cheap and extremely potent high, though very dirty and brain-altering. Mexicans at a meat packing plant sixty miles to the east were said to be a current source of trafficking, but there had been plenty of Legion locals making their own batches, too, including a high school teacher's son who several years earlier had accidentally burned down his parents' house. People were reluctant to believe it then. Now they mentioned the bad smell associated with its manufacture. "Ever get a whiff of it at your house?" they asked. "Like super cat piss?"

No, I was glad to say, no super cat piss for me. My place had been thoroughly cleaned out; and though I now understood that the new sink and bathtub were less an expression of my landlord Mr. Simms' decorating sense than of legal constraints (a meth lab was considered a toxic waste site), it was actually quite pleasant at my farmhouse on a sunny morning as light flooded in and I ate honey on toast and listened to birdsong through the screens. The country was beautiful. Everything was just fine at Stanley Acres. Until, one morning, a brisk breeze blew from the north, and I discovered another kind of odor problem.

A sewer stench that seemed to drift, improbably, out of my trees.

This was about a week before I bought the motorcycle. After I closed my windows and gathered my papers, I went out and stood by the side of the road and waited for Russell's school bus. Soon I began to press my shirt against my face.

Holy shit, I thought, what *is* that? It was coming from my orchard—no, beyond. It made my eyes squint. Could somebody's fertilizer be that bad? Jesus, is it possible? Shit. *Shit. Shit!*

It was truly gasp-awful: a septic bomb. Asking around at school that day, I was told that the stench came from a hog lot on the other side of the river.

"Are you sure?" I said. "That would be miles away. There are pigs closer to my place and I can't smell them from my kitchen. It couldn't come from so far."

I'd seen some spotted sows and piglets along the school bus route. Cousins of Bernie, I'd supposed. They lived in little structures that looked like tin teepees.

But no, it wasn't so simple.

"You haven't heard of the Double Dee?"

The Double Dee, they said, was a series of confinement buildings next to huge lagoons of liquid shit. Even if you couldn't see the animals, you could smell them from afar. The odor depended not only on the wind but also on the temperature and humidity. Evidently Mr. Simms hadn't thought to mention it.

"An operation that size produces as much sewage as a town of 100,000 people," said a kindergarten teacher with liver lips named Chadwick. He blinked whenever he spoke, and wore scratchy-looking shirts that were so tight around his chest that you could see his nipples. "Some neighbors have had to move out."

"Listen, they've brought more new jobs to this district than anybody you can name," said Mrs. Gordon. "Who gives the most college scholarships to our high school seniors? And I'm not just saying that because my husband Roger works there, I'd say it even if he didn't. Soon they'll have the new visitors' center—you'll see what they do—and it'll clear up a lot of misconceptions. Without their taxes we'd have layoffs in the police force, and in the schools, too. People would move away and you younger guys might not have a job."

It seemed like a touchy issue, so I changed the subject. But now I understood: my paycheck was linked to shit. Fortunately the wind didn't often blow strongly enough from the wrong direction that I had to think too much about this connection, though the day I strapped my duffle on the back of the Yamaha 650 and rumbled down the road to escape to Chicago for a weekend, I noticed, with a sniff, that once again the air was getting a little too *conspicuous*.

☾

My PLAN in Chicago was to see a woman named Beverly. She was a divorced nurse whom I'd met in a North Side pub when I was waiting on the paperwork for my temporary teacher's certificate. We'd shot some pool and hit it off pretty well, and she'd told me that it was too bad I was going away, that we should keep in touch. "Sure," I said, while thinking that it was too impractical because of the distances involved and that nothing would come of it. Then, after a few lonely weeks of TV at the meth house and after I got hooked up to its old dial-up internet connection (which was impressive for its grinding and moaning sound, as if I were tapping into purgatory), we started exchanging emails. This made a big difference. Soon we exchanged several messages per day. Eventually I got a short and direct email in which Beverly suggested that we sleep together.

Count me in, I replied. *You called that right.*

For a whole week this invitation boosted my spirits and made it easier to get through my workdays in Legion. It felt, in a welcome way, as if the wheel had turned.

We agreed to meet on a Saturday night. On Friday, after teaching all day and then enduring a long, ass-numbing motorcycle ride, I arrived late at Riley and Serena's place. Their boys were in bed and there was a subdued atmosphere in their house as they tiptoed and spoke softly. It was a big house, doors were closed, but more than once they told me to keep my voice down. I must've been partly deaf after five hours of straddling a roaring engine. One of the first things I learned was that they were expecting another child.

"Congratulations!" I shouted.

Serena smiled and winced at the same time, as Riley leaned forward. *"Shhhh."*

They served me a frozen tiramisu. "It's low-fat," Riley reassured. "You know, Speck, maybe you've figured it out, going back to the country. You're a step ahead of the game." He levered an enormous wedge onto my plate. "Serena and I are thinking about relocating, too. Someplace clean, no crime. That's worth a lot nowadays. We've done pretty well these last few years, but that's no great feat, the way the economy was till recently. People were throwing money and you just had to stand there and catch it. But that's not the only thing, is it?"

I took a forkful, and tried to look thoughtful. (*Some of us must not have been standing in the right place.*) I was still in debt and felt embarrassed by the laughably small check I'd brought along to give Riley as partial reimbursement of the money he'd lent me. My first earnings had gone into getting established in Legion and buying the motorcycle—the wad of money from the shed hadn't covered the entire cost—and, at this early stage, I was still far in the hole. Riley hadn't pressured me about paying him back; he hadn't even mentioned it, probably didn't care; so maybe my concern was a matter of exaggerated pride. For his part, Riley spoke about the future of his family and the twin evils of terrorism and taxes. "I'd like to be able to offer my kids the kind of environment we had growing up," he said. "That's what it comes down to, Speck. Once you have a family, you have to think about these things."

"I'm sure you do," I agreed, remembering how eager he'd been to leave our small town when we were kids. It was surprising to hear him wax nostalgic. Our father had died young, after which our mother had gone through a series of loser boyfriends and enough other problems to fill a sad little book. It wasn't particularly wholesome. Now I changed the subject by quizzing him about our mother's latest romance.

"Are you sure this Archie guy is okay?" I asked. "I'm supposed to have brunch with them tomorrow. What's he like?"

"He's no looker but he's not a drunk or a cannibal." Riley shrugged. "Far as I know. Mom seems head-over-heels. I haven't seen her react like this to a guy in years. It could be the real thing. He has loads of frequent flyer miles and he takes her places. She likes that."

"I think he's very considerate," Serena said. "That counts for a lot."

Later, when we said good night and I retired to a guest bedroom, Riley came along to show me how to operate the towel-warmer in my bathroom (he'd just bought the gadget and it had a timer and a number of settings which allowed a person to regulate the toastiness of a towel for that crucial moment of stepping out of the shower and rubbing one's body); and, after I'd washed and used my prewarmed towel and lay in bed with the lights out, I was uncannily aware of the objects around me: the matching cherry wood nightstands on either side of the bed, their brass lamps, a double chest of drawers, a large television with a red standby light, glowing like a dragon's eye. All these *things*. And my brother wasn't showing off: his state-of-the-art towel-warmer came as naturally to him as buttoning up a fresh shirt. You had to give him credit; Riley had done well for himself. But why did I feel so cramped and oppressed? Was it jealousy? Or was something deeper wrong with me?

I pictured the bareness at my farmhouse, the lack of furnishings there. Yes, that was more restful. Perhaps, after all my years of traveling, I'd lost the habit of possessions. The ability to bond with objects. That in itself didn't bother me—but something about tonight's claustrophobia of *things* perversely made me all the more aware of what I did truly miss, and what perhaps I had squandered so far in life, in my embrace of immaterial dreams. Delphine had tried to be good to me. There had been other women, too, from whom parting wasn't easy but was always justified by my future plans. But what were those plans now? What was my future? Things or dreams didn't work. People—only people—you could be good to. That was home. So far I was nothing.

❦

THE NEXT morning began with a phone call from my mother at the emergency room, explaining that Archie had experienced an extreme nosebleed on his exercise bicycle and had had to be rushed to the hospital to get himself cauterized. "He's going to be all right," she reassured, "it just got awful messy. Can we do our brunch another time?"

"Of course. No problem."

So, before starting my weekend with Beverly, I had extra free time on my hands. After declining an offer to join Riley at his sons' soccer matches, I spent a pleasant, leisurely morning at the aquarium, admiring various scaly monsters. Then, as prearranged, I stopped by Beverly's place in the afternoon. She thought the motorcycle was fun; she climbed on behind and hugged me (here we go, Beverly, yes!) as we buzzed along the lakefront, a beautiful, crystalline fall day. Then we parked and went for a long walk along the lake, holding hands. We looked at the boats and, avoiding the crowds at Navy Pier, found a peaceful place called Leo's for coffee and cheesecake.

"Do you play a musical instrument?" she asked. I told her no, but she smiled and shrugged and accepted this information. There was a pause in the conversation as we watched people in the street pass by our window. It wasn't an awkward pause. We were just resting. Our day was going well, and we both knew it. "When we're together online that's fine up to a point but it gets cramped and even trivial," she said. "Isn't this so much better?" I nodded, and she pushed aside her cup. "Say, would you like to go to the aquarium? It's not far from here. That's always fun."

- 47 -

My hesitation was brief. I didn't want to spoil the moment or dampen her enthusiasm. What did it matter if I'd already gone today? Why mention it? "Sure," I said.

So, a short time later, we were walking down softly lit corridors among the tanks, a world of colorful sea cucumbers and marine worms. We avoided the most popular exhibits and the groups of squealing children; instead, we sought out our own more tranquil, adult way, communicating mainly by smiles and nods. Our shoulders often bumped together. On occasions when we did speak, I appeared very knowledgeable, since some exhibits were fresh in my mind. "Hmmm, could that stingray over there be a whiptail?" I asked as we approached a tank that I'd seen a few hours earlier, where a dark, otherworldly creature with white spots on its dorsal cruised eerily along a coral reef bottom. "I do believe it is."

Beverly bent to read the plaque. "Wow, Stanley, you're right."

Later, we dined at a Greek restaurant and ate flaming cheese. Twice in the course of our conversation she asked me if I was already married or in a relationship—this seemed to concern her, because she didn't want to spend time with a guy who was cheating—but I was able to tell the truth *and* please her. (How about that!) As I spoke I was careful, as I'd been all day, to show her my left profile, away from my black eye, which had mostly healed, but I still preferred that she see my good side. That night, and not too late, we went back to her apartment in Rogers Park.

"I felt weird about asking you to sleep with me," she said. "But I also had a good feeling about you."

"Thanks," I said. "You've been terrific. I've had a great day."

But as she prepared a pot of herbal tea and began to lay down the ground rules at her place, I realized that there had been a misunderstanding. Because that was all Beverly wanted—just sleep. Not sex.

"I like to get at least nine hours on weekends. The effect is salutary. There's a fun diner not far from here where we can have breakfast tomorrow. If you want—"

"Excuse me. Wait a second. Did I hear you right? No sex. That's what you're saying?"

She looked me in the eye. "Yes, Stanley, that's what I'm saying."

This definitely gave us something to chat about over tea. I tried to persuade her to reconsider, to get her to *talk* about sex, to get her in the spirit of things. (*I* was in the spirit of things.) But to no avail. She said, "If that's what brought you here, I don't have time for you. Actually, if sex was a club, I wish they'd cancel my membership."

"Why? What do you mean? How can you say that?"

Beverly sighed.

"I'm not saying sex is bad. But it gets attention way out of proportion and attracts creeps. Know what I mean? You're willing to be nice to me, right? A cuddle is pleasant, that would be fine, but no sex, Stanley. If the arrangement doesn't suit you, I understand, but then you'll have to go elsewhere. *Do you understand?*"

It was all too clear.

"Then let's just cuddle and sleep together, okay?" she said.

A short time later I climbed into bed with Beverly, and it was weird and frustrating. She asked me to face the other way, whereupon she hugged my back against her breasts and stomach. Like on the motorcycle but now we were so still. *This* was the shared comfort she desired. "That's nice," she said. "Yeah, like that. Good night, Stanley."

"Uh, good night."

Even with my back turned I could feel her softness, her warm breath tickling my neck. My thoughts raced, and soon I throbbed with other possibilities. My erection bunched up uncomfortably in my underwear. (This was another house rule: T-shirts and underpants were obligatory.) "Don't wiggle," she whispered. "Just stay still." She held me in place and, before long, her breathing was slow and steady.

I clenched my eyes shut. Was this the way to be good to her? I don't know how long I lasted. But sleep was out of the question and eventually I turned around and tried to touch her.

She awoke grumpily. "Hey, cut it out."

She pushed my hand away.

"Beverly, I've got something for you."

She groaned. "Oh, Stanley, just stop."

"But you can't be serious! It's like the wheel has turned!"

"Huh? I don't know what you're talking about. I was straight with you. You promised!"

"So I'm supposed to just lie here like an anatomically-correct teddy bear?"

She made a little click in her throat. I waited for her to say something, but this was her only answer.

"Beverly," I pleaded. *"Beverly . . ."*

But nothing. So I turned around and we resumed our original position; she held me in place so tightly that it affected my breathing. Beverly was one strong nurse, I can vouch for that.

3

"**D**eke! Deke!"

The Homecoming football game, a crisp night under a ragged yellow moon. Shortly before kickoff, the team captain, a blond boy with improbably broad shoulders who everybody called Deke, led the team in warm-up calisthenics in the end zone. The grandstands buzzed. The boy paused, put on his helmet and attached the chin strap. There were scattered whistles and cries and, in the crowd, rubber Bernie noses were being passed around.

"I got an extra one if you forgot yours," Chadwick told me.

"Thanks."

I hadn't intended to sit next to Chadwick but he'd waved to me from a lonely perch in the upper bleachers and it would've been a statement to snub him. It was as if he'd been waiting for me. Probably most of Legion had turned out, and among the faces I knew I saw Mrs. Gordon, sitting next to a tall bald man who must be her husband, Roger; Mr. Worthington and his family; and, further on, Nelson the art teacher in the company of a little girl with glasses. I didn't see Jim or Christine Snow, or Shana Linn, but I recognized plenty of my own pupils who roved in packs between the sidelines and concession stand. Their parents were surely among the spectators sitting with Chadwick and me, the adults who turned around and openly stared, sizing up The New Guy. Soon we would meet face-to-face for our first parent-teacher conferences, and tonight was like a preview. I'd been absent from other scheduled activities for Legion's Homecoming Week because I'd fallen ill with a cold and insidious earache and missed work for two days. ("School is a germ factory," Nelson had said, "every rookie teacher gets sick. Never fails.") But, by the end of the week, I was back on the job and felt obligated to show up for the game.

"I'm glad you made it here," said Chadwick. "This'll be a good chance for us to talk." There was an unmistakable hint of purpose in his voice. "How would you like to join us at church this Sunday? Have you heard of the New Tabernacle? We are all fellows in Christ. If you come along, you'll see what I mean."

For the rest of the pre-game ceremonies, Chadwick told me about the New Tabernacle. His wife was its pastor, and it was the fastest growing church in Legion. This fact, he explained, created jealousies, especially with the older denominations. Chadwick had been a lapsed Methodist himself until a few years ago when he'd been converted by the woman who would become his wife. Members of the congregation came from all backgrounds and walks of life. "The Xicays, you know their girl, right? The Guatemalan family?" He pointed across the crowd to where one of my pupils, Ester, sat with her parents. Chadwick explained that the Xicays had started out as Catholics but had been persuaded to join the New Tabernacle. A Mexican family from nearby Brewton had done the same. This had rankled members of the Catholic parish.

"Mrs. Heffernan—you know, the person whose job you have now? She told us we were poaching. She'd always been active at St. Anthony's. It got pretty tense there for a while but then she got sick and that put everything into perspective. Why have hard feelings? In the end it's about love."

In front of us, a marching band moved across a green grid-marked field, brass horns glinting in the floodlights. It was the first time anyone had said anything negative, however mild, about my predecessor, who still cast a shadow in this place. Mrs. Heffernan had been diagnosed with lymphoma last spring and it turned out to be very aggressive; her death over the summer and her conspicuous absence at the beginning of this school year had made a forcible, unhappy impression on my colleagues. I was still introduced sometimes as "Mrs. Heffernan's replacement" to people who politely shook my hand while seeming to look past me, remembering *her*. It was nothing personal, but at a certain level I was an unwelcome reminder of mortality. When no one came to claim the cartons with Mrs. Heffernan's name on them, I'd persuaded the janitor, a bandy-legged man named Les, to take them away. For all I knew he dumped them in the trash. Other items in my classroom, such as signs in Mrs. Heffernan's handwriting and colorful picture postcards from appreciative pupils, still decorated the walls. I left them in place because it saved me the trouble of putting up my own decorations.

"What about church this Sunday?" Chadwick persisted, and touched my arm.

I shook my head, and then pointed. "Hey look! It's Bernie!"

A young pig was running on the football field, followed by a spotlight. The pig was draped in a banner of the school colors and some boys loped alongside it, guiding it toward the home bleachers. The crowd cheered encouragement as the pig trotted up a ramp to the podium at the fifty yard line. I half expected it to make a speech.

"Somehow I'd pictured a Bernie as bigger," I said.

"It's not a Bernington, it's just a young gilt," Chadwick said as the marching band broke into the school song with a rush of trumpets and a trombone whoo. "She's got a lot of growing ahead of her."

Spectators affixed their rubber pig noses, tilted their heads back, and let loose squeals of anticipation.

❧

"Do you live in the country?" the doctor asked me.

"Yes." But I didn't add, *"At the meth house, if you must know."* Instead I wondered: What's that got to do with anything?

"Your digestive problems could be linked to the water you drink. Do you filter your water?"

"No."

"Does your place have a surface well or a deep well?"

"I have no idea."

He bobbed his eyebrows at me.

"From what you tell me, that would be the first place I'd look. I've seen a number of cases like this. You'd better drink bottled water, or fill up jugs here in town. Don't drink out of the tap."

"You mean it's not safe in the country?"

"For pregnant women especially, it's off-limits. There's the nitrates, and when we get some hard rains and the other run-off, I don't think *anybody* should go near the stuff. Did you have this problem before you came here?"

"No."

"What water were you drinking?"

"A lot of Chicago city water, actually. Straight out of Lake Michigan."

He smiled. "Well, when all is said and done, that's probably a safer bet."

So I followed his advice and, sure enough, within days my condition improved. I drank only the water at school, which was heavily treated and tasted and smelled like spray deodorant, or I guzzled from big gallon jugs purchased in Leroy's Supermarket. Leroy's wasn't the sort of place to sell fancy designer waters in sexy liter bottles. It came exclusively in large sizes, which seemed to influence my consumption. I drank huge quantities, trying to flush out my system. When I was alone at school and not slipping out of my classroom to relieve myself between lessons, I jumped up and caught a piece of exposed pipe on the ceiling and did pull-ups, tugging on the school brain like an unexpected thought.

❦

CRABAPPLES POKED out of the leaves like pink fingertips reaching for the sky. Beneath the tree, the ground was littered with bitter fruit that was feasted on by yellow jackets. Boys ran daring missions and dodged the yellow jackets and scooped up the fruit, which they threw against the side of the school. Sometimes it stuck.

We were waiting for the bus. My motorcycle was in the repair shop, so today I was back where I'd started on the first day.

"Hello there!"

I walked over and sat beside Jim and Christine Snow on the school steps, where ants crawled from crack to crack.

My arrival was unexpected but this time Christine hesitated only slightly before returning my greeting, while Jim merely nodded and looked down. He obliterated an ant with his thumb.

In search of conversation, I began to tell them about my recent motorcycle accident. "Happened right here in town, caught me totally by surprise. I'm lucky to be alive."

This last statement was a gross exaggeration, but I wanted to get their attention. And sure enough, they both locked me in their gaze.

"*I thought I was a goner,*" I continued . . .

The truth was less spectacular. The accident had occurred after I'd done my shopping at Leroy's Supermarket. Probably I shouldn't have strapped six one-gallon jugs of water to the motorcycle, which no doubt affected my balance, but I did a careful job of it and drove away in perfect confidence. Then, I took a corner—my speed didn't seem excessive—and hit a patch of pea gravel. As sudden as a sneeze, the bike shot out from between my legs. It happened so fast that I didn't believe it at first. The next thing I knew, jugs were rolling in all directions and I was bouncing on my rear end and watching my motorcycle skip down the street on its side. Sparks flew out each time the motorcycle scraped the pavement and, for all I knew, from under me, too. As I bounced along Legion's Main Street on my ass, I remember thinking with absolute lucidity: *How long can this last? This suck sucks.*

"The front fork got bent bad," I told them. "I'm still pretty sore. A person has to watch out."

They nodded solemnly.

"We got bikes," Christine announced.

"Mine's fast," Jim said.

"Hey Jimbo, come here," someone called.

Jim wiped his thumb on his jeans and regarded the group of boys who stood near the crabapple tree looking up at a baseball cap. Someone had thrown it in the air, and the branches had caught it. A boy jumped and jumped to pull it down, but he couldn't quite reach it.

"Jimbo! Give us a hand."

Slowly he shook his head.

"Come on, dude, you're tall. Get over here."

He turned to Christine. She touched his arm and somehow I felt it too, this warning pressure, which said *ignore them*, and she looked down the street. The bus was nowhere in sight.

"Jimbo, let's go! Hey!"

They were warm, they were friendly. I didn't trust them for an instant.

"We need you, dude. You're bigger'n us."

The pleas increased and suddenly Jim found himself the center of attention—and this time, they weren't jeering. They wanted him. They *demanded* him. Jim gulped, as if to swallow his disbelief, and walked down the steps.

"Yeahh!"

Christine called to him but he didn't stop. He continued toward the cheers. Boys slapped him on the back and led him to the tree. When he turned around, he was smiling.

"Atta boy Jimbo! Go for it."

He jumped but didn't reach it. He tried again, collecting himself for the effort, and then springing, but he was a poor leaper. His feet barely left the ground.

He shook his head, when suddenly a small boy jumped on him and, as swift as a monkey, climbed up his back and onto his shoulders. Jim didn't know what'd hit him and he stumbled forward to keep his balance. The boy rose up on

Jim's shoulders, and together they swayed, they teetered. Jim latched onto his ankles to hold steady. The monkey reached into the branches and plucked the cap. He threw it: the cap went spinning off into the sunlight. A breeze caught it, carried it away, away. The crowd of boys chased after it, yelling and waving their arms at the sky. The cap sailed on. When I looked back at Jim, I saw the monkey had jumped off him. He grabbed Jim's belt buckle and yanked, turning Jim around, stripping the belt out of his pants. Jim clapped his hands on his hips: too late. An instant later, the belt cracked across his shoulders. Jim cried out, staggered forward.

"Hey!" I shouted.

The belt snapped again, aimed at Jim's legs, and now the boy ran away, laughing, waving the belt above his head like a captured snake.

I shouted once more, but he paid no heed. Jim began to pursue him. Farther ahead, the cap drifted down, the boys tumbled after it, falling on the ground and each other. They wrestled for the prize. Jim ran as fast as he could, but he was already falling behind.

One boy, the champion of them all, stood up and slapped the baseball cap on his head. He saw Jim chasing the thief: he laughed, pointed. The other boys, who were pulling each other to their feet, began to hoot and whistle. The thief loped over to them, still waving the snake belt above his head. They all cheered.

When Jim finally caught up with them, they formed a circle around him. I'd jumped down from the steps and now strode briskly toward the scene. The boy with the belt held it out, dangling it just beyond Jim's reach, and Jim lunged—missed it—as the boy jumped back. The boy darted and feinted, left and right. Children hurried along with me to watch the fun. In seconds, it seemed, the circle in front of us had become swollen with spectators. They howled with delight at the sight of Jim lurching across the space like a drunken bear. "*Get it, Jimbo! Come on, you fag!*" The belt was swinging, it hissed through the air. I saw Jim lunge again, I took another step, and I remembered Billy Snow, the day he'd raced through the garden and plunged into the cornfield. I saw him disappearing, his legs swallowed up in green.

The belt buckle caught the sunlight: a glint, like the flash of a fang.

I pushed forward. "That's it! Hey, hey! Knock it off! Right now!" The boy saw me and stopped teasing; he looked beyond me and dropped the belt. He backed into the circle. All was quiet. I looked at Jim. He lowered his eyes, panting; he clutched his arms in front of himself, as if awaiting a shudder so he could wake up.

"What's going on here?"

It was Shana. A wave of children fell back from where she stood. She stared at us with cold green eyes, and Christine held her hand. Christine's face was flushed with splotches.

The children shuffled their feet in silence. No one dared to answer her question.

"It got out of hand," I said, scanning the crowd for the boy who took the belt. "It started as a game—"

"Get back in line!" she told the children. "Your bus is coming."

The children obeyed, dispersed, and left us standing there. The belt lay in the grass. Christine picked it up.

"So you're just standing around and watching?" Shana said. "What on earth is the matter with you?"

She glared at me.

"Wait a second. I'm only here by accident. You see—" I was going to say more, but Christine returned and I checked myself.

"Never mind," Shana said.

She stepped toward me, gave me Christine's hand, and walked away. She knelt down to Jim.

I couldn't look at her. I felt the moistness of Christine's palm. At that moment, I hated them all.

☾

"Have a cigar," Nelson said.

I declined.

"Come on. They're bona fide stinkers."

I took the fat brown cigar and sniffed it because that's what people always did. He called to the bartender for two beers. He lit our cigars and clapped his hand on my shoulder.

"Tonight," he said, "let's drink until blood comes out of our ears."

I had never seen him so jolly, so expansive. He puffed and smiled, a round face of geniality in a cloud of smoke. After school today he'd invited me down to his art room and we cooked pizzas in his kiln. Now it was getting late and we sat at The Sportsman's Corner, a bar on the Legion town square.

Gently, he clinked his glass on mine: "Cheers."

I asked why he was so jovial. "Are you celebrating?"

"Not really. In fact—" he sucked on his cigar, "I'm feeling a little depressed, so I treat myself. Sometimes I like to go out with a friend and cheer myself up."

I looked down at my smouldering cigar and wondered why he'd chosen me. He pulled out a wallet and extracted a card. "I'm going through a divorce," he said. "I don't know if you know. I have a little girl, Andrea, and she starts school next year." He pointed to the card. "Turn it over."

I turned it over, and it wasn't a card, it was a photograph. A little girl who was sort of cute.

"Keep it," he said.

"Thank you, but you'll want it back . . ."

"No keep it. I've got dozens of them. They bring me good luck."

He ordered two more beers. I hadn't finished my first yet. "You were at the football game with her," I said. "I saw you there."

"That's right. She comes for the weekend. She's quite the little pistol."

He told me about Andrea as he drew designs on the bar with his forefinger. Their last time together they'd gone camping and she'd worn a plastic football helmet and butted trees. She collected birds' nests and had started a fire all by herself. She'd been diagnosed as nearsighted but they'd found glasses that didn't make her look too serious. Recently he'd learned—the news came as a blow—that her mother had taken a new job and was moving to a St. Louis suburb, and she'd started proceedings for full custody.

"It's complete bullshit," he said. "But I have to answer to it, and prove what's already been proven. You don't know what it's like."

He was right, I didn't. And from the tone of his voice, he seemed to find it a shortcoming in me. I wanted to say something that would return him to his previous mood, to the joking, cigar-chomping Nelson. I looked at the picture and said, "She's a pretty child."

But this increased his melancholy. He examined my face, suddenly became shy and looked away, as if he'd said too much. He picked up the photograph and held it like a wafer between us. I wished he'd put the damn thing away. After a pause, he reached forward and inserted it into my front shirt pocket.

My cigar had gone out. I felt the rectangle of the photograph against my breast. Now it was my turn. I had to give him a sign, a proof of our friendship. I was mystified about what I should do, and for a few seconds flirted with the idea of not being his friend. Frankly, I wasn't eager to earn his trust. But he needed me. It wasn't enough to hold his beer, his cigar, his photograph.

"You're not the only one," I volunteered, rubbing the back of my jeans. "Since I became single again and moved to this town, it's been a bumpy time. And what can you do? Take this place. Look at all the women here!"

I made a sweeping gesture—my point was, there were no women to be seen, just a few fuddled geezers hunched in a booth. There wasn't much to recommend The Sportsman's Corner except as a place where you could study drunks in their natural habitat.

Nelson narrowed his eyes at me.

"Well boo-hoo for you," he said, none too kindly. "You got no kids, right? Unattached, is that what you're saying?"

"That's right."

"You're just a loner with a boner." He picked a speck of tobacco out of his teeth. "That's easy enough to fix."

"You got me figured out, do you?"

It occurred to me what a crash he would make if I kicked his stool out from under him.

"No, I'm not saying that. Only remember: you're not in the game forever." Nelson gave a queer grim laugh.

Our conversation almost ended there, but I wasn't going to leave my drink unfinished, and by the time my glass was empty, we'd found other subjects, which led to more drinks. I complained of my money problems, of how the insurance company might not pay for the damage to my motorcycle, and he continued talking about his ex-wife, of complicated schemes to thwart her on a property settlement. The man was obsessed.

Over his shoulder I watched as a burr-headed guy, who'd entered a few minutes earlier and now sat drinking a can of soda at the end of the bar beneath the sign that said *We Support Our Troops*, was met by a young man in a flannel shirt. This young man didn't order anything but gave a nod to the burr-headed guy, and they both moved past the pinball machines and out the back door. There was nothing out there, I knew, just the dumpster. Nelson kept talking. A short time later the burr-headed guy returned, alone. He saw me watching him and stared back in a challenging manner, so I looked away. The next time I glanced in his direction, he was gone.

Nelson and I closed down The Sportsman's Corner that night. The bartender unplugged his neon sign, told us to leave, and we reached for our jackets and struggled to our feet. We waddled toward the door.

Outside, a scratch and the sudden flare of a match: Nelson lit another cigar, and I noticed for the first time that he had a handsome face. He extinguished the match, walked on.

"Soon they won't let us smoke in bars anymore. New law, my friend. Tonight'll be just another golden memory. Hey. Come here."

I followed the sound of his voice. The sidewalk was uneven and I stumbled.

"Shhh. Be careful."

He peered down an alley, and I came closer, remembering the burr-headed guy.

"How about that," he said.

He was looking at a curled-up dog. The dog was white and seemed to glow in the alley dark with eerie electricity. Nelson studied the animal, but the dog was too preoccupied to take notice of us.

"Do you know why a dog licks his balls?" Nelson asked.

I rubbed my nose. Was this a joke I'd heard before? I thought for a moment, and then Nelson spoke for me:

"*Because he can.*"

The dog wagged his tail feebly, and twisted himself harder. He whimpered.

"But you see Stanley, we can't! We can't!"

For an instant it seemed that he wasn't joking but was saying something elemental, even profound. But then the instant passed and it was only more raving. I told him, "Come on. Let's go home."

He didn't say anything as he drove me in a rattling, dusty Nissan, and my thoughts drifted to facing work in the morning, to the imperious bells, the many cups of coffee that would be necessary to get through the day, the rabbity face of Ginny Rawlings. When I climbed out of the car, he called across the front seat, "Remember, Stanley. I'm always here to help."

☾

DURING THIS period when I was back to riding the school bus, sometimes we would pass a police car parked on the edge of the road, and a policeman walking in the ditch, looking at his feet as he waded through weeds and tiger lilies. According to my school colleagues, he was in search of cough formula bottles and empty antifreeze cans, on the trail of methamphetamine cooks. In the litter he hoped to find incriminating evidence. I never found such signs around my house—or more cash, either, though I admit I poked around, hopefully—but, early one evening, I had an unexpected knock on the door.

On the other side of the screen was a woman I didn't know.

"You're not Kenny!" she said when she saw me.

"No. Who's Kenny?"

"Don't bullshit me!"

Her hair hung limp on the sides of her face, and she barked out her words. Before I had time to reply, she suddenly shifted her expression, rounded her lips into a wet **O**, extended her tongue and then languorously sucked it back in. "I'll make it worth your time," she said.

"Who are you?"

Her expression shifted again, to distrust. She whirled around and stomped back toward her car, where someone was waiting in the front seat. For a moment I thought this person was trying to duck low and hide, and then I realized it was simply the round head of a child, barely above the dashboard. What the hell? I wondered. As the car lurched out of my yard and sped away down the road, it became obvious to me that this knock was about meth, and she was looking for the previous renter of this place. Sorry, lady. No Kenny here.

During my bus rides, I was also glad to see that there were no further incidents of heckling Jim and Christine Snow. I liked to think that this was due to the kids actually experiencing some remorse, and not to my policing presence.

Still, it was unlikely. These children weren't as simple as I wanted them to be. They'd surely been teasing and getting their wrists slapped for a long time; their excitable, mean little faces were all too fresh in my memory. Now, when the Snows got on the bus, they were greeted by dead silence. Was this another kind of game? Relations had flipped, it seemed, to another extreme. Jim and Christine became ghosts in a crowd of children.

The silence felt unnatural, as if it were waiting to be broken. One morning, as we bumped along, I tried to learn more from the boy beside me. He had chubby pink cheeks and was sipping on a can of soda.

"What do you think of them?" I asked.

"Who?"

I tilted my head toward the front seats. He paused, looked at me sideways.

"Oh, Jimbo, Christine. They're okay."

He leaned back and looked out the window at the cornfields, as if to drink them in. He took another sip.

"Why do you call him Jimbo?"

He shrugged. "That's his name. He's a big guy. Jimbo, like Jumbo. You know."

"Do you like him?"

"Can't say. Don't really know the guy."

"Why won't you talk to him? Or Christine?"

"Why should I? What have I got to prove?"

☾

INDIAN SUMMER. On a warm Saturday afternoon in October I hiked along the river, stopped and stuck the fishing pole I never used in the mudbank. I ate a sack of sandwiches beside the slow water and thought of Shana Linn. For a time we'd stopped speaking to each other, but recently the chill had lifted because I'd mentioned the problem on the school bus and told her that I'd fixed it. This was stretching the truth, of course, but at least this story seemed to please her, and make her friendly again. Now, if I could find a touch of—

Voices upstream interrupted my thoughts. I heard laughing and splashing.

I extracted my fishing pole and approached with a light step. I peered through the gooseberry bushes along the bank. First I saw the flash of an arm, long and shiny in the sun, like a fish jumping. Then I saw their faces: Jim and Christine.

They were naked. Their clothes hung in the bushes like shed skins. Christine leaned back in the water and floated, her long wet hair drifting around her. Occasionally a big round knee or a big round breast would bob above the surface. Jim was treading water; he bounced up and down in a strange way, as if he were twelve feet tall and his feet could touch bottom. He squirmed and splashed, and flashed his arm at me again.

I didn't want to interrupt, but I didn't leave them, either. I stayed and watched. They were playful. Jim skimmed the water with his arms and sprayed Christine, who churned the water with her legs and splashed back. They laughed and blinked and snorted the water that had gone up their noses.

I would've thought swimming in October too chilly, even on a day like this. And I'd never seen them so relaxed, so removed from the school world. Yet the more fun they had, the more uneasy I became. I thought of Jim on the school steps, raking her back with his fingers. I thought of the school bus kids and their razzing. Maybe they knew something I didn't know. Possibilities, bizarre and perverse, ran through my mind.

And I kept watching. A lavender dragonfly flitted around them.

Eventually they got out of the water. Only then did I realize that this was what I'd been waiting for. Christine's big white body glistened in the sun; water ran in rivulets around her flesh. Jim had a lanky body of pale yellow, a long skinny penis, a dark slit for a bare bottom. They shook themselves and coughed. Then they began to pull on their clothes.

And as quickly as the idea had come into my mind, I understood that I was wrong. They stood with their backs to each other, both respecting an unnecessary privacy. They were casual yet shy. Brother and sister.

I had to get out of there. I slipped through the gooseberry bushes, trying not to make noise, and I cut myself in the bramble. My head hurt. Was it the sun, or somehow my conscience—but I hadn't done anything wrong, had I? Yet I felt guilty. I looked up. There, in a catalpa tree, sat Billy Snow, shirtless, his legs dangling. He waved shyly. I hurried downstream with my fishing pole.

4

Parent-teacher conferences brought a parade of people I wasn't keen to meet, a first reckoning and a recognition of my responsibilities to the community. Mainly people wanted to be reassured about their children, to be cheered on—an understandable sentiment, of course, though it was odd that they should put so much trust in *me*. Sometimes both parents came: the soft-spoken and beseeching Carters, who made it very clear that they were *concerned*, although their daughter Lisa was well-behaved and did excellent work and was at the top of her class in most subjects. The Carters hovered around for more than their allotted time and put me behind schedule for the rest of the evening. The Morehouses, in contrast, seemed fairly satisfied by the mediocre performance of their son, Randy, a cheerful nosepicker who lived a block from the school and spent hours outside of class in his front yard on a trampoline, bouncing up and down while cradling a BB gun in his arms. Next in line were Ester Xicay's parents. Mrs. Xicay was a little woman with a crown-like braid and she asked all the questions. She worked at a day care center run by the New Tabernacle church and was comfortable in English, while Mr. Xicay, a housepainter and part-time employee at the Double Dee, looked on and nodded from time to time; I couldn't tell how much he understood.

For most pupils, though, only one parent came. Invariably, the mother. Mrs. Rush was easy to get along with. Although I wasn't fond of her son, Brain, our conference went smoothly. I let her do all the talking and she agreed with herself. Evan Willoughby's mother was shy and surprisingly young, and looked barely out of high school, while Aimee Anderson's mother told me, not too diplomatically, that her daughter would've been better off with my predecessor, Mrs. Heffernan. "She was a very good teacher—everyone says so. And now this class gets stuck with the job of breaking in someone new. It puts them at a disadvantage."

"Yessss . . . I see what you mean."

Ginny Rawlings offered the most delicate case. Mrs. Gordon had pulled me aside to warn me about her family situation. "Ginny stays with her grandmother now. She was living up in Des Moines, but her father has been in and out of detox and her mother thought it would be a better environment for her down here. Her mother grew up in Legion before she went off to college and married this guy. He's a real estate developer, there's lots of money in his family. Last spring, Ginny's mother came home early one day and found him in the garage trying to gas himself in his car. Ginny was in the house at the time, watching cartoons. He was going to end it all, just like that, with Ginny there. I got this straight from Ginny's grandmother. Anyway, that's when her father went into detox and Ginny came down to Legion."

"What kind of detox?" I asked.

She grimaced. "Crystal meth. Even a guy like that."

I nodded as if I understood. *Even a guy like that.* I wasn't sure exactly what she meant, but I think it had something to do with his status. Apparently, for Mrs. Gordon, if this successful guy had been an alcoholic or cocaine abuser it would've carried a different stigma than methamphetamine. In addition to being more dangerous, meth was supposedly a low-class thing. A step down in the pecking order of fucking yourself up.

Ginny Rawlings was a weak pupil but she hadn't caused me any trouble. A quiet girl, she set herself apart from classmates who were bigger and boisterous. She rarely volunteered in class and, when I called on her, she inhaled sharply and looked down at her desk and sometimes wiggled her feet as she tried to come up with an answer. As if she were pedaling toward a destination she couldn't quite reach. From the beginning, I'd had a minor prejudice in her favor because she was a left-hander like me, and she needed, for instance, to sit at the end of the craft table. In a world of sharp elbows, we lefties had to look out for each other.

For the conference, I fully intended to say agreeable things about her to Ginny's grandmother. Ginny's poor academics didn't matter as much as the fact that the kid didn't seem screwed up. That was the main thing, wasn't it?

But the conference didn't go as I'd expected. Instead of the grandmother, a petite woman in a navy-blue suit with matching pumps clip-clapped sharply across the wooden floor toward my desk. She extended a hand. "Good evening, Mr. Mercer. I'm Amy Rawlings. Please know that I'm here to listen, and I'm counting on your candid assessment of Ginny's progress."

I asked her to sit down. Her formality seemed faintly ridiculous but I have to admit that it intimidated me a little, too. Even before she introduced herself, her stylish appearance had made a statement. Other parents were more casual, some parents had bad teeth and bad grammar and wore Bernie baseball caps. Ty Carson's dad had brought along a two-liter bottle of Mountain Dew, and unscrewed the cap and drank from it during our conversation. People in Legion weren't inclined to put on airs. Amy Rawlings took a chair and sat up very straight in front of me.

I lowered my eyes and began to read out some of Ginny's scores. (In truth, there wasn't any "progress" to speak of.) Still, I explained, even if Ginny hadn't done too well in Reading or Math, there was every reason to believe that she could improve . . .

"Excuse me," she interrupted. "What's your method?"

My method? I leaned back in my chair and cleared my throat, stalling for time, knowing that I ought to be able to answer this question even if the fact was, I didn't have a method beyond following the curriculum and copying the grey-haired lady down the hall. Every night in bed I read the textbooks to brush up on the material I'd forgotten, often discovering facts

I'd never known. (Walruses lived to be thirty years old! Their whiskers grew out to twelve inches!) Preparation took up a lot of time: the cookie-cutter lesson plans that came with a textbook's teacher's manual almost always had to be adapted. Amy Rawlings watched me, waiting for an answer. I would have to brazen this out.

"Which do you mean?" I asked, looking her directly in the eye. "Language or quantitative? And you should know that I put plenty of emphasis on interdisciplinarity." (This last was a word that I'd heard tossed around at in-service meetings.) "I prefer projects that are transversal."

"Look, that's fine by me. But it depends upon how it's done, of course. You know what I mean."

I nodded. I didn't have a clue.

"I realize that it's not easy," she continued, "I really respect the professionalism of educators, but because Ginny's education is priceless, it's incumbent on me to be vigilant . . ." She went on in this vein, watching me fixedly, and briefly I wondered if she was putting me on, being sarcastic to my face. But she didn't blink or miss a beat and I understood that she meant business.

"Well, Mr. Mercer. I must be on my way." She stood up abruptly. "I believe this gentleman wishes to see you."

In the doorway, a slope-shouldered man in a plaid work-shirt stood watching us, waiting his turn. She offered her hand for me to shake. It was very small, plump, almost childlike, and when I squeezed it, the gesture felt flirtatious, and dishonest, as if I were agreeing with everything she said. Still, I let my hand linger. Suddenly I wanted her to understand me, a desire that I knew—even then!—could come to no good.

☾

TUESDAY, AFTER the final bell, I saw Christine being taunted. In the hallway a boy was poking her in the ribs, beneath the line of her brassiere. Christine backed away but he followed her, poking. I approached them, wondering why she didn't say anything, or slug him. She would've been more than his match. As I drew nearer, I heard him speaking in a low voice. *"What about it, Christine? Do you like boys?"* He poked her. *"Do you like boys?"*

He probed the space between Christine's breasts. I seized him by the collar, turned him around and pushed him up against a locker. The metal behind him banged with a sound much greater than the force I'd actually used. Fear swirled in his face, an alarm that surprised me. Only seconds before I'd imagined him as a tougher type, but he was just a kid, a squirrelly boy with a smudge of fuzz above his lip where he was trying to grow a moustache.

"You can't touch me," he said.

I released my grip.

"Get out of here," I told him. "You'll have to deal with Mr. Worthington for this."

He hurried away, and when I turned to Christine, she was already leaving in the other direction.

"Wait a minute. Are you all right?"

"Yes, yes."

Her hands were trembling. I wanted to take them and say everything was all right; I wanted to apologize for the boy. I wanted to apologize for the world that made her be Christine. But that wouldn't help. She knew too much. She was afraid of me, too, and she turned away, shoes scuffing down the hall.

I went to Mr. Worthington's office. He wasn't there. I checked the halls and the teachers' lounge without success. Then I glimpsed him ducking into a restroom. I followed him, and saw his feet in the last stall. He wore wing tips.

"Mr. Worthington?"

"Are you speaking to me?" said the voice in the stall.

"Yes, I am. We have a problem."

The wing tips skittered in irritation. The voice said: "Oh, can't it wait?"

"Yes, but not for long. I'll be outside."

I stood in the hall with folded arms and eventually heard the flush and rush of water. He appeared with a worried look on his face.

"Well?"

I explained the situation, and he said *um* repeatedly, giving little sniffs. It was known that he suffered from allergies and it was impossible to tell what he was thinking.

"What are you going to do about it?" I asked.

He thought for a moment, and then said, "You haven't written up a bullying incident before, have you? I'll give you a hand with the paperwork. But if he says you pushed him? Did you?"

"*Touched* him. Barely. I was stopping him."

(I was pretty sure he'd heard me right the first time, but he was double-checking my version.)

"Any other witnesses? Other students? Anybody get photos on their cell phone?"

"No."

This seemed to please him. He told me that he'd email me an attachment of a form I should fill out, and that I should call him if I had any questions. "Don't leave any blanks. We'll get through this. Don't worry. Martin usually stays out of trouble. It doesn't sound like she was hurt."

"Well, not physically, at least. But that's not the point. Shana's kids put up with no end of indignities."

I listened to myself and imagined that Shana could hear me.

He sighed. "Oh, spare me. It's no worse here than anywhere else. I'm trying to help you out, in case you didn't notice."

Then he walked away.

What the hell? This wasn't what I'd expected, so I decided to go and see Shana. As I approached her classroom, I saw Jim and Christine come through the door, and I remembered the day by the river: I imagined them naked. I blinked to dispel the image. I entered the room, feeling off-balance.

"Ah, a new student!"

Shana sat at her desk. On shelves and windowsills were a number of uncarved pumpkins. We laughed and I sat down.

Although I'd come to tell her about the incident with Christine and my conversation with Mr. Worthington, her friendly mood affected me, and led to a change in intentions. It happened quickly. Shana was wearing a green top that I liked, the one with pearl buttons down the front. I decided that the subject of Christine could wait.

"I think it would be nice if we got together," I said, launching in directly. "Outside of school, I mean, and go have dinner somewhere, just us two. Would you like to do that?"

She didn't answer. She picked up a pen from her desk and clicked it several times, then put it down and looked at me. She seemed more surprised than pleased. Now I found it difficult to look into her eyes but I forced myself, because if I didn't it would seem I was looking at her body.

She reached for me, taking me by the elbow. "Come here," she said. "We should talk."

I pulled my chair beside hers, and felt the touch of her fingers more than I heard her words.

"I think I can trust you," she said. "I like you."

I said nothing, waiting for her to go on. Was this Yes?

"I haven't told anyone at work," she said, "because we both know what kind of town this is. I need my job."

I didn't know what she was talking about, but her face was close to mine. And I thought: *The kids are out of the way. I could kiss her here.*

"Tell me," I whispered.

"Privacy is hard to come by in this town," she said. "Mrs. Gordon, for instance, she drives me crazy. I've caught her snooping around my room. It's nuts."

"I'll be discreet," I assured her, and leaned closer.

She blinked and pulled away, startled. She tried to cover her surprise but it was too late. She shook her head.

"Wait a minute. Thank you for your invitation, but I have to tell you: I'm not interested in men."

I nodded automatically.

She touched my arm. "I want you to understand," she said. "I'm interested in women. One in particular."

"Oh," I said. "I see."

She gave my arm a squeeze, as if to extract a larger response. Suddenly I felt more disappointed than I'd imagined possible. A surging desperation, in the manner of my kids who, once they were denied something, wanted it more still. I said, "Well, I'm glad you told me. It certainly simplifies matters."

"You think so? But Patty Gordon—she makes me nervous. For a long time I've thought I'd feel better if I told someone here at work. I keep putting it off when I know I shouldn't. People assume I'm single. That's the easier card to play. Everyone here is older and more traditional, you know."

"Shana, you can count on me as a friend."

I suppose I meant it, though I still wanted to kiss her and undo her buttons.

She said that her girlfriend Carol came to Legion almost every other weekend, and that I should meet her. Carol was a great cook, she told me, and recently she'd returned from Morocco. She was making a documentary on the famous Blue Men.

Now I looked at my watch. Because it was time for me to go. "Sorry, Shana. I have a bus to catch."

℃

THAT NIGHT I marked a pile of schoolwork and labored over the form Mr. Worthington sent me, after which, feeling wound up and not ready to go to sleep, I went to my living room and began pacing. A short time later I zipped up my coat and left the house.

Above me was the cold white incandescence of the stars. Hiking down the dark country road, gravel underfoot, I listened to the sounds of open space, which traveled easily on the crisp autumn air. I heard a dog crying a mile away, and coyotes yipping closer by. The lonely nervous bleat of a sheep. Then, the wind picked up, and an unmistakable odor met my nostrils.

I turned around and jogged back to the house, where I picked up the telephone and tried to call Delphine in Paris. This was not an inspired choice but I had to talk to *somebody*.

It would've been seven A.M., her local time. My mind was full of images of our snug little apartment on rue Lavin—*her* apartment—the phone beside the bed, the old brown beams overhead, the first light creeping in the skylight . . .

Ten. Twelve. *Twenty* rings.

She wasn't home.

I put down the phone and walked several circles around the room. No, I didn't want to think about this piece of information. For a moment my hands quivered at my sides, and then I picked up the phone again and called Beverly in Chicago.

When I heard her voice, I hesitated.

"Who is this?" she asked.

Should I hang up?

"Is this Binky?" I asked.

Binky was the name in Beverly's email address, which I'd used numerous times in the heat of correspondence.

"Who is this?" she repeated.

Now I laughed, and tried to make a joke out of it. "It's Stanley. Didn't you recognize me? How are you?"

"Oh, Stanley!"

To my surprise, Beverly was pleased. She explained that she was up at this hour because she was making custards. It was a favorite nighttime interlude. (Okay, I thought—whatever.) "I've wondered about you," she said. "Have you wondered about me?"

Our conversation flowed, and it was almost enough to make one forget the circumstances of our last meeting and our problem with sleeping together. Tonight she chatted and chatted, moving around on her cordless phone, and I listened to the background noise of her working in the kitchen and then clearing away and filling her dishwasher. Soon she was getting ready for bed. I told her my own story while she brushed her teeth.

"You going to stay in that little town?" she burbled. "Excuse me, I got to spit."

"I don't know, Beverly. It's not fun and games but I can't walk out on my job, can I?"

"I guess not."

"You want to come visit me?"

We spoke in circles for a while, and then she was in bed.

"What are you wearing?" I asked.

"My Bears jersey. I'm number 88."

"Uh huh. Got something underneath?"

"Why? What do you mean?"

"Are you wearing underwear? I'm just curious."

"Like, scientifically? I don't know why you do this, Stanley. We were having a perfectly nice conversation, and now this. Sex is in your head."

"No it's not. I mean yes it is, but not only *there*. That's the point of my question."

"Why can't we just talk?" she asked. "Why is that so hard? It ought to be easy."

"Do you think I'm a pig?"

"Don't get mad. I'm only saying . . ."

"It's okay," I interrupted. "I understand. I understand."

☾

I'm in the bus. We turn down the rutted lane and I see that the rabbit cages are open, the doors yawning on their hinges. Russell is driving fast, too fast, down the lane. We bounce and jostle from side to side, picking up speed. The children begin to whoop it up. In the driver's seat, Russell leans back, relaxed. Through the windshield I see the lane is teeming with rabbits. At least a dozen of them, fat and waddling, black and white, nibbling the green that grows between the ruts and taking lazy hops.

Russell does not slow down. The rabbits make no attempt to move until the bus is directly upon them. Then they explode, jumping in all directions, some of them panicking and bounding toward the bus. When this happens, children cry out. Jim and Christine sit in front, on top of it all. I hear three distinct thuds, one after another, like snowballs pelting a metal shed. The left rear wheel goes over a bump. Finally, the bus skids to a stop.

The doors pop open. Jim and Christine hurry out. And for the first time in weeks, the kids repeat the ritual. "Bye Darling Christine! Bye Bye Jimbo!"

I unclench my fingers from the seat in front of me.

"Hey!" I shout. "Knock it off!"

"Jimbo, Jimbo, Jimbo!"

I make my way to the front of the bus. "Stop it!"

And at last, they do. I turn to Russell and say, "This is crazy. What's going on here?"

He looks at me but all I see is my own reflection in his sunglasses. He doesn't answer. Hurrying down the steps, I want to speak to Jim and Christine. But they've vanished. Where did they go?

I woke up at the clack of a mousetrap. It took me a few moments to realize where I was. The source of the sound. I'd caught another.

I got out of bed and put on some clothes, and then took the little grey corpse outside and threw it over the fence onto my mouse pile.

I heard the telephone ringing and ran inside. It was my brother Riley. "How's things?" he asked.

"Weird," I grunted. "It's weird here."

"What do you mean?" he asked. "You got it made, Speck. The peaceful country life. O beautiful for spacious skies. Play ball! Health and sunshine where the tall corn grows."

"Oh, knock it off."

"I'm serious. I wish I could come to the country and relax, get away from the escalators."

"Really?"

"Yes, man, it's tough here."

So I urged him to visit me, and his voice trailed off as he said he might. Then he asked,

"What are the people like there?"

"They're fine," I said. "I'm starting to fit in."

"What about women? Or are you still chasing after that nurse you met here?"

"A little. But I'm seeing someone local, too."

"You horny rabbit. Go for it. What's she do?"

"She's a teacher, too. Special education."

"I should take a page from your book," Riley said. "Get down to basics."

I squeezed the telephone and took the easiest step of all, saying, "*Yes?*"

NOTEBOOK TWO

Amy Rawlings

5

I got a Pontiac. That's when everything started changing fast, when the game broke open. On a raw November day I answered an advertisement on the bulletin board of Leroy's Supermarket and rode my motorcycle to a farm on the other side of the river. The farmer was friendly; he wore gum boots and waved with a yellow glove as my engine rumbled to a halt and an enormously pregnant dog waddled forward to inspect me and sniff at my tires. The dog had a lolling tongue like a slab of ham and a huge flat head you could've balanced a glass of beer on. I scratched her ears and she moaned. The farmer shook my hand, saying the Pontiac was in the machine shed—a pearl he called it—and then backed it out for me to see. We chatted while he washed off the bird shit with a garden hose. He seemed pleased with my company, as though he hadn't spoken to anyone for a long time. He said the car had been idle for half a year, but now he'd decided to sell.

Speaking to him, I felt a little strange. The name on this advertisement, in neat, hand-printed letters next to the telephone number, had been *Roy Heffernan*.

Or maybe it wasn't strange. Legion was a small town, after all. But should I call him? What should I say to the guy?

Or was it necessary to say anything? It was only a matter of business. The weather had turned chilly and commuting to work on a motorcycle was getting pretty uncomfortable. It was time to take measures. I'd already answered some other ads for used cars but hadn't found what I wanted. Why exclude this possibility? So I'd made the call, set up a time. Our meeting took place the day before Thanksgiving.

"You're not from around here, are you?" he asked as I stood beside him. He turned off the nozzle of the hose. "What do you do?"

It sure hadn't taken long for the subject to come up. Anonymity wasn't an option in this town.

"I'm a teacher. Actually I'm the one who replaced your wife at the elementary school. This must have been a very hard year for you. I'm sorry."

He looked past me and was silent for a moment. In the nearby barn lot, fat black cows munched on hay. A few lifted their heads and stared at us, while others strolled through the muck, dropping piles that splashed and steamed. Then he nodded. "I've heard of you. But I didn't connect the name. Here." He held out the keys.

We took the Pontiac for a test drive on the country roads, and in the car Roy Heffernan became talkative, as if he wanted to control the conversation and steer it away from the subject of his wife. "Go slow," he advised as the windshield wipers blip-blapped and the heater blew warm air on my neck. "A soupy road like this'll suck you right into a ditch." Visibility was good across the recently harvested fields and Roy pointed to the sights along the way: the dead elms where he hunted for mushrooms each Spring; the old windmill where a fellow he knew had lost two fingers—truly lost them, they'd gone flying off into the weeds and were still out there, somewhere; the empty farmhouses where the Caldwells used to live, the DeGoeys, the Schobers.

"Interest rates in the eighties ate most of the little guys alive," he said. "Now these places belong to big farmers who really cover ground. These guys aren't as diversified and they got big-time equipment, too. People can't afford to be small anymore, not in the old way. They work a job in town, too, and maybe keep some livestock on the side. Or they make stuff on the wrong side of the law."

"Do you raise pigs?" I asked.

"Hogs? No. I'm in beef. Angus, some Charolais. This is the big hog place coming up right here. This is the Double Dee."

We approached a cluster of metal buildings and machine sheds. I'd left the window open a crack to dispel some fog on the windshield, but now I closed it against the stench.

"Who lives here?" I asked.

Roy laughed. "*Live?* People work here, but nobody lives at a place like this. Would you want to smell that night and day? Pull in and turn around, I want to show you something."

I slowed down and turned into an asphalt lot, where half a dozen vehicles were parked. The grounds were neat and well-tended, with ornamental shrubs. A huge, whirring fan stood at the end of each building.

"This place is state of the art," Roy said, as I maneuvered the car around. "Farrow to finish. Those hog houses are climate-controlled. Heated in winter and air-conditioned in summer. Not a hog sees the sun, ever—it's like how dopers grow hemp under lamps? 'Course, hogs aren't as hardy as cattle. In a confinement operation where they're all packed in, you got to baby them a lot, they sicken easy." Roy pointed. "Go back that way."

We back-tracked a quarter of a mile and then he told me to pull into an equipment lane. "Don't go far, you'll get stuck." We came upon a rise of land, and then looked down the slope.

"There's the lagoons. See?"

In a weedy pasture was a large cleared space with banked-up dirt and more shrubs, encircling a line of open cesspools. For one of them, the color of the contents was a surprising neon pink. "That's the other side," he explained. "That's where all the hog waste gets pumped. Quite the swimming hole, eh?"

I had no idea why he was showing me this, but it seemed important to him. He leaned over with his windburned face and expected a reaction.

"Can't they use it for fertilizer or something?"

"You kidding? A fraction of it. I've seen it get sprayed, even when there's snow on the ground. But where are you going to put all *that*? Think of the phosphorous."

I nodded, pretending to weigh the question. What the hell did I know? Mainly I was struck by the stillness of the place. It was hard to believe that we were in the presence of thousands of animals. We drove on, making a loop or, more precisely, a plotted square, since these roads respected the original surveyed section of prairie. Even when the terrain and landmarks were unfamiliar, the geometric exactitude of these roads kept a person from getting too lost. That was how the rolling landscape had been framed. We turned a corner, and it began to sleet, popping against the windshield. I felt warm and secure inside the Pontiac, distant from the slush and struggle outside. The steering wheel shivered against my hands.

"I'll take it," I said.

Back at Roy's house, in his kitchen, he removed a coffee can from his cupboard and rummaged through papers in search of the Pontiac's title. He spread the papers on the table. "You can leave your motorcycle in my shed and come back for it another time, if you like. The weather's getting nasty out there." I wrote him a check, ripped it out of the book.

"This title is in my wife's name, but I still sign for her," he said, clearing his throat. "It shouldn't be a problem. We were married for thirty-nine years, three months."

Then he bent over the table. His pen squeaked on the paper, and it seemed intrusive to watch too closely, so I looked away. Of course I still heard the sound: the last echo of her name, which he no longer said aloud in this kitchen. There was something ghastly about this moment. Surely there were photographs of Roy and Nancy Heffernan together in the living room, or upstairs beside his bed. I thought of his solid arms around her.

"Here," he said, pushing the paper toward me.

I picked it up, and he led me to the door.

Outside it was dusk, the light looked dirty. On my way to the car I was startled when something brushed against me. I jumped—then saw it was the dog. I patted her big head and got in the car, started the engine and jolted away.

𝒞

THAT NIGHT, I drove and drove. First I'd taken a dead person's job, and now I was driving her car. Borrowed goods, borrowed time. Nothing belonged to me, no more than the darkened landscape I was passing through.

Recently I'd consented to let Nelson store some of his furniture, including supposedly valuable antiques, at my place because he wanted to keep them out of the hands of his ex-wife. "She's contesting the inventory of the settlement," he'd said. "No way is she gonna get this stuff. I'll pay you, Stanley. This is serious."

I'd consented. Why not?

Now I eased off the accelerator and imagined the rumble of buffalo that had sounded on this same prairie.

A few days earlier, I'd stood in the meth house kitchen and tried to call my mother about the holidays. It was time to sort out plans. Unexpectedly, a man's voice had answered. For a moment I froze, thinking I had the wrong number. "You want Ruth?" the man wheezed.

"Why, yes," I said.

The man turned out to be Archie. It was the first time I'd spoken to him.

"Oh, *Stanley!*" he cried, "Sorry we won't see you for Thanksgiving, man, but I had a terrific deal on tickets to South Padre Island. All inclusive, we couldn't pass it up! You know, I've heard a lot about you."

"I've heard a lot about you, too." For a moment my mind went blank. Then I recalled, "Uh, you sell frozen concentrate, is that right? How's business?"

"I keep the juices flowing!" A gasping laugh, vaguely obscene, came through the receiver. "You gotta connect, Stanley," he said. "That's the trick. That's the secret! Don't forget it."

Now I stepped on the gas again and my Pontiac plunged through the darkness and I pictured myself as if from above, a dot on a drifting continent. I recalled Archie's advice, and said out loud, *"You gotta connect, Stanley."*

☾

For Thanksgiving dinner I went to Shana Linn's and met her girlfriend Carol. It had been friendly of them to invite me, but on the whole it was a fairly stiff occasion where we ate too quickly in the dining room and then retired to the living room, where we sat around and looked at each other and drank microbrew beer out of fancy foiled bottles while pretending to say clever things. Carol was a graduate student in film studies at the University of Minnesota, a very young-looking blonde with a fresh-scrubbed face. (My first thought: Shana had robbed the cradle.) When Carol learned that I'd lived in France, she brightened immediately. She was eager to talk about the Cinémathèque and various expositions which, unfortunately, I hadn't seen. When I mentioned the Paris Buffaloes, she was taken aback.

"Baseball? Over there?" She laughed. "What happened—did you get lost?"

"Not exactly. The Buffaloes are a sort of novelty, they played exhibitions against private athletic clubs. Over there it's a rich man's game for French people who've traveled and think it's chic. They want something different. The Buffaloes represent the sport, do clinics for kids, whatever brings in the money. A sort of Wild West Show."

Carol let out a high, nervous cackle. Somehow what I said didn't fit with what she knew, and it discomfited her. But she tried to be pleasant and the conversation loosened up when we turned to local subjects, such as the Snows and the administrative warning Martin Donnell had received for harassing Christine, and the problem Shana was having with kids driving by her house at night and throwing beer cans and other trash on her lawn. Weekends were especially bad, and if she happened to be away, she returned to two days' accumulation.

"Homecoming was worst of all. They were honking and shouting abuse at all hours. At first I just tried to ignore it, collected the cans and took them in for the deposit. Then one day I picked up a can and discovered that someone had cut it open and stuffed a dead rodent inside—maybe a mole, which seems like a lot of trouble to go to—and had waited until it was vile and had begun to rot. When I lifted the can, this maggoty ooze poured out and ran straight down my sleeve. It was awful! About made me sick. I called the police after that one, to complain, but unless there's actual property damage, they just shrug it off as kids' pranks. They have other priorities."

"And there's the mailbox, too," added Carol.

"More moles, dead birds. Dog shit. I took it down. Now I just rent a post office box. It's the easier option."

"But what's their point, really?" I asked.

They both sat up a little straighter, and I realized that it was a foolish question. Shana said quietly, "To express their feelings, Stanley. What else?"

IT WAS still early when I left Shana's place and, since I didn't want to go straight home, I went to The Sportsman's Corner, half-hoping, half-dreading, to run into Nelson.

He wasn't there, but I spent a few hours drinking way too much draft beer and watching college football on a wide screen TV with a burly man named Scotty who checked his cell phone every three minutes for messages that didn't come.

The bartender surfed half-heartedly on a laptop computer balanced on a rear counter; he was connected, after a fashion. But visibly bored. At the jukebox a young guy flipped through the music selections, back and forth, but he didn't put in money and play a tune; he just kept flipping, flipping, as if the process was an entertainment in itself. He did this for at least an hour, mesmerized. You could wonder about his brain. The Sportsman's Corner wasn't the most charming place in the world to spend Thanksgiving, but it was a holiday, after all, and we had to get through it.

Eventually I told these friends good night and went out to the parking lot. I was in no condition to drive so I proceeded very slowly, grateful that there were no police in sight, stopping at Jaycee's convenience store for some gas, because my gauge was almost at Empty. As I stood at the pump, listening to the barely audible tick-tick of numbers on the digital readout and gulping down the chill night air, I noticed a woman pacing on the narrow walk in front of Jaycee's, talking into a cell phone. I enjoyed watching her, her movement in snug black jeans. She was lost in conversation but, even so, she had a certain strut. I stood there, teetering in the gas fumes, thinking: *Yes, waggle that pert little ass.* At this stage of the evening, that's where my mind was.

I replaced the nozzle, screwed on the gas cap, and went inside to pay. As I passed the woman, suddenly I recognized her. From my parent-teacher conferences. It was Amy Rawlings.

She paid no attention to me but as I waited for change at the cash register, I continued to watch her in profile through the plate glass windows. She wore no coat, just a fuzzy black sweater with silver streaks. She'd done something different with her hair since the time we'd met at school. Bangs, that was it. A fringe dangled and brushed against her eyebrows and, as she spoke on the phone, she stuck out her lower lip and expelled air and blew up these bangs. She did it a second time. Then she snapped her cell phone shut.

I pocketed my change and went outside, pausing a short distance from her, looking out into the night. I cleared my throat. "Happy Thanksgiving," I said.

She burst into tears, slapping her phone against her thigh.

"Hey!" I said. "What's the matter? What is it?"

"Go away!"

Her reaction was incomprehensible, and I stood in silence, trying to think of something to say. She turned her back and clutched her arms in front of her. She was sobbing, and when I drew closer, she said over her shoulder, "Didn't you hear me, creep? Go away! I'll call the cops!"

I stopped. For a moment I was going to walk away and go home, but something made me hesitate. Her distress was real. So I lingered a moment longer. "Don't you remember me? I'm Ginny's teacher."

Her back straightened. "Oh God." Now she turned around, taking in deep breaths, wiping a palm on her face, trying to regain her composure. "Excuse me." She looked me up and down. "What's your name again?"

☾

WE WERE sitting in my car, parked on a side street, talking. She hadn't wanted to stand in front of the gas pumps at Jaycee's, and I hadn't wanted to drive around in my condition, so I'd told her it was easier for me to listen if we were stopped. She didn't seem to mind.

"I stalked out of Colleen's and I shouldn't have done that but I couldn't take it anymore. I came down here to spend Thanksgiving with her and Ginny, and instead of having a nice holiday dinner and sharing good company, Colleen kept needling me. She did it right from the start when she saw I didn't bring pie like I said I would. But she'd fixed all this food, a crazy amount, more than we could possibly eat! She needs to lose weight anyway. But that doesn't stop her from needling me about the pie and about a bunch of other things, too, and she knows that after a certain point something like this will happen, and it upsets Ginny, too, but she won't stop. She won't let up. She needs to get a life."

She slapped the dashboard—her tears were gone, and now she was simply angry.

"Is Colleen a friend of yours?" I asked carefully.

"She's my *mother*." Amy laughed bitterly. "And doesn't everyone in this dinky-ass town know it! So I storm out of there and this just upsets Bughouse more. Bughouse—that's Ginny, sometimes we call her that. But I go out to my car and turn the key and get this—*the car doesn't start!* I can't believe it. The engine doesn't even turn over. The battery's dead. I must've left the lights on or something. Well I'll be damned if I'm going back in the house and there's not the slightest chance that Colleen is going to lend me her car, anyway, so I just started walking. Couldn't stay there another minute. I tried to call my friend Debbie to come and get me but she's an hour-and-a-half away and she was really grouchy because it's stupid Thanksgiving and she's with people and doesn't want to budge from the table. Today is just a *nightmare*. I guess that was when you saw me. Holidays suck, don't they? They always have. Why do people even pretend? Or maybe I'm just being rude. Is that how you spent the day? Hanging around a convenience store telling people, 'Happy Thanksgiving?'"

Now I laughed. "Not exactly."

We talked for a long time. We alluded to the need to find somebody with jumper cables but then the conversation moved on. She spoke of Ginny, and said she came down to see her as often as she could. She told me that she'd gone to college in the East and now she ran a clothing boutique called Tivoli's at the new mall near the interstate, north of Legion. "I like being my own boss. That's the way I'm wired. I don't have to put up with anybody's bullshit."

Her tone was very different from our conference at school. It was almost like talking to another person, except there was the same self-assertion, which now seemed to be passing through a different filter. This time Amy Rawlings didn't seem so pompous; she was sharp-tongued and lively, a little raucous. She asked me if I'd been to the new mall or seen her store, and when I said no, she started quizzing me. "Why did you come to Legion? What does a teacher boy *do* in this peewee town? There's nothing, believe me. I about went nuts here when I was a kid."

As I described my job, rambling on a little, suddenly it struck me how sad and sweet Amy Rawlings looked. Sure, my perceptions were far from reliable at this point. It's pretty certain that she wasn't *feeling* sweet. But that was what I saw and, on an impulse, I leaned across the seat and kissed her on the mouth.

She didn't push me away but when I let up, she looked up at me, squinting.

"What's that about?" she said directly. "You don't know me."

I was sort of surprised myself, and since I wasn't sure how to reply, I did it again—kissed her broad, soft mouth. A very desirable mouth.

This time, she moved away after a few seconds, but she didn't say anything against it, and resumed talking about Legion. She told me about the people who used to live on this street in a voice that was a little different now, lower; I took her in my arms, but she tucked her head and assumed a new angle that would make it difficult to kiss her again. While she spoke, I began to stroke her hair. Eventually she pulled away, laughing softly. "Hey, come on. What is this? We're not teenagers in daddy's car."

"I know that."

There was a silence, and I reached over and gave her hand a squeeze. She had very small hands, I remembered from earlier. I let off squeezing but could not bring myself to release her hand; she let me hold it, and for at least a minute we sat in the front seat, looking straight ahead into the darkness. Then, with my finger curling up and under, I slowly began to circle the soft part of her palm. I pressed, and then circled the other way, and then paused. I was very aroused. Somehow it affected me more than a kiss. It was the first time in memory that merely holding hands had had such a strong effect on me. I sensed a change in her breathing, too. It wasn't my imagination.

"It's late," she said softly.

"Let's go someplace," I said.

Eventually she answered, still more softly, "Okay."

❧

AT THE meth house (where else could I take her?) I showed her the way upstairs to the bedroom. I'd tried to put my arms around her and kiss her as soon as we came in the door, but she slipped away. Now she asked for a towel. While she was in the bathroom, I sat on the edge of the bed and kicked off my shoes, trying to focus. When she returned to the bedroom, she dropped her towel and quickly slid under the covers. I didn't stare, but it was hard to pretend to be nonchalant. I went to the bathroom to wash up and brush my teeth, going through the motions, blinking out my contacts. I found a condom which I palmed discreetly, hoping that when the time came, I wouldn't fumble too much.

Back in the bedroom Amy punched her pillow into shape. I dropped my towel and slid in beside her. Then I turned off the light.

The darkness seemed gratuitous, since we'd gone this far. Strangely, it undercut our boldness and made us shy. We reached out, embracing slowly, pausing. One of us should say something, I thought. But neither of us did. We let the silence surround us, and limit us. I began to rub her along the length of her body; she did the same to me. My hand drifted down her backside. She stiffened, my hand stopped, and she made a sound, a tiny cough. She held me tighter. Her hand had risen to my shoulder, where her thumb clamped down. Her grip was not encouragement; it was more like resignation, steeling herself for a test. I felt the pressure of her thumb and had

– 91 –

an impulse to pull away, escape the situation. But there was no place to go. My erection, which had returned between us during our embrace, faltered. It melted away.

"Maybe we should talk," I said. My voice was strange; I didn't sound like myself in the dark.

"It's not that easy," she said. She turned her head, speaking to the ceiling. "We really don't know each other."

A mouse scrabbled in the plaster. I almost laughed out loud. Then what the hell are we doing here? I thought. In fact I would've laughed but for another question: How are we going to extricate ourselves? This was a delicate question, requiring tact. The most sensible solution would be to call tonight a mistake and forget about it, avoid complicated explanations. Wouldn't that be best? But that would require a big dose of self-assurance from both of us, not so easy at this moment in the dark. To be in bed was to be in deep.

The sound of the mouse grew louder. Scratching.

"You have animals in your attic?" she asked. "Raccoons?"

"It's only a mouse," I said.

"How can a mouse make so much noise?"

We listened for a while to the intricate footwork, until suddenly the sound stopped. The room was silent except for our breathing. I felt sleepy, and wanted simply to say Good night. Why shouldn't we? It had been a long day. Maybe we could just hold each other, for comfort. (*Beverly*, I thought, *if you could see me now . . .*)

"I think it could be nice if you made love to me," she said. "But it has to be gentle. Let's just relax. And be gentle."

She touched me. I was far from excited, at this point, but I felt obligated to do something, I had to respond. She turned on her side, so I slid an arm under her and we embraced, kissed. I couldn't muster much feeling. She became bolder, touched me in a seductive fashion, but I was slow to get started.

"What's the matter?"

Her voice was defensive.

"Oh, I'm just a little nervous, that's all."

This wouldn't do. My eyes had adjusted to the darkness, and I could discern the outline of her face. I tried to think of Beverly. There wasn't a strong resemblance but it was possible to pretend. I kissed her mouth, concentrating on the image. It made all the difference. Soon I took out the condom, luckily got the damn thing right the first time, then reached down and stroked her gently, circling, teasing a little. She was dry. So, I'm not the only one, I thought, and then I slid down and kissed her between her cool white legs. She had a pleasing taste; I stayed there a long time. I could tell it soothed her. It soothed me, too; I began to think of her as Amy again.

I rested for a moment, rubbing my cheek on her thigh. I hoped Amy was thinking only of me, too. I wanted it to be me. I resumed, tracing my lips between her legs, across her lips. Then I kissed her deeply. Her legs began to shiver. I kissed her again, deeply, and she arched herself against my mouth, pressing. I stayed with her, and her hands came down to clasp my head, holding me there; she rocked back and forth. I tasted her completely. *Amy.* Her legs trembled, first closing over me, and then opening up again.

We slipped once, but regained our rhythm without difficulty, gave ourselves to it, and the rhythm was getting better all the time, we did not stop, we kept going until we reached a point when the rhythm was not enough: she spread her legs widely and pulled me up, my lips sliding with her wetness up the length of her body, across her stomach and the swollen tip of a breast, until she kissed me hard on the mouth. My penis swung over her thighs, long and awkward, I dipped this way, that way, till she caught me and, with her guiding hand, directed my thrust into her cleft. Once inside, I made myself stop; this was the pause I liked best. But not for long—suddenly I pushed in—she was so slick that she took the length of me in one stroke. I pulsed, almost came at once. I concentrated for control; I stirred myself, and her, slowly. Her hands assisted the motion, and soon it controlled us, as thoughtless as breathing.

We went faster, then slower, playing with it, but eventually I felt myself straining beyond retrieval. Amy still needed more time: she was reaching, not quite there. I tried to wait; I brought my face to her face, her cheek was hot, and I pressed my mouth to her mouth: I tasted a trace of her wetness there. Immediately I emptied into her, the sensation broke. Amy must have realized what was happening, because she lifted herself against me and stayed there, holding fast, until it broke for her, too; her shoulders shook but she still held on.

6

"Our friend the pig came over to the New World with Columbus. The pig was right there with conquistador De Soto, too, when he discovered the Mississippi. In 1609, at the first settlement in Jamestown, Virginia, the pig came along with Captain John Smith and, by golly, did he prosper! Historical records show that less than twenty years later, the people at Jamestown had to make barriers around the town to keep the pigs out. Today America is the biggest pork producer on the planet. Right here in Iowa, we've got nineteen million hogs to three million people. Stop for a minute and think about that! Nowadays we call pork the other white meat. It's lean and it's clean and it's healthy. Did you know, not long ago I read that the Chinese word for pig differs only in tone from the word for Jesus?"

Roger Gordon spoke with authority at the visitors' center. A tall man in a stitched down jacket and handsome boots, Roger wore steel-framed glasses that gave him an intellectual air. I couldn't help noticing with a pang of jealousy how well he held the kids' attention. Even Brain Rush was absorbed and respectful. This field trip took place on the Tuesday after Thanksgiving, and though I was careful not to show it, I was particularly aware of Ginny Rawlings in the group, of where she stood and how she reacted. She paid no special notice to me.

Now Roger called our attention to the farrowing crate behind him, where a large dozing sow with distended teats nursed nine or ten piglets which poked their snouts through an adjoining crate. Roger deftly retrieved a piglet, which didn't squeal as I expected; rather, it emitted a rubbery squeak like someone twisting a balloon. Then the piglet fell silent. Eyelids half-closed, it panted a little.

"He's a nice one, isn't he? We keep the little guys separate from mama because mama is big and if she rolls over, she might squash one of her babies."

The children laughed. "Big" was an understatement. This sow was *enormous*. She reminded me of a giant larva, almost six feet long and maybe half as wide. There was just enough room for her to lie on her side and allow the litter to nurse. When she managed to rise to her feet, she would be able to move one step forward or one step back. It was impossible to turn around. Her spindly little legs were largely irrelevant appendages, like incidental growths, no longer of use.

Roger brought the piglet forward and immediately the kids wanted to hold and pet it. You couldn't blame them. It was a curious thing. What was it about a baby pig that was so appealing? In comparison, human infants were grotesque little creatures.

"You want to give him a name?" Roger asked, and the children responded with obvious suggestions like "Pinky" and "Snorkler."

This visitors' center was a neat and pleasant place, eight miles from the Double Dee's main facility. It was part of the company's public relations outreach. Roger told us, "I'll be frank with you folks. It can be stinky in the big barns." He pinched his nose, and the children laughed again. "But the main reason we have you visit here is that the big place is a working operation and we have to think about safety. Safety first! Not just yours, but the hogs, too. Some of you might live on farms yourself and bring in sickness from your animals. So we're careful. Our facilities are just like what you see in this hog parlor, only bigger. Nice and toasty, isn't it? Our hogs don't get chilled."

It was true that the temperature was a comfortable change from the chilly outdoors. With the metal pens gleaming in the overhead lights, the place didn't remotely resemble a drafty old barn. I tried to imagine the pens multiplied by hundreds—thousands? The children, however, were focused on the piglet.

"Do you have any Berningtons to show us?" I asked. "I've never seen one."

He smiled. "No, sorry. You're not likely to see a Bernington. That's just a bit of folklore from way back, not a real breed. Around here hog farmers have worked with Hamps or Chesters or Durocs, mainly. There's mixing with the boars. About every third cycle or so they'd bring in new gilts, or hang on to some gilts and breed back. That's nothing new. Your market hogs are crossbred."

I had no reason to doubt him, but I still wanted to see a Bernie. He seemed downright mythical. The kids were unconcerned. Roger told them that as world population approached nine billion, demand for food would soar and America, and especially Iowa, would play a big role in feeding the planet. People needed *us*. It sounded daunting but flattering, too. At the end of the tour they jostled eagerly to get a free Double Dee cap. Now all their heads looked the same.

𝐶

"How was your Thanksgiving break?" Nelson asked. "I took Andrea to the Ice Follies."

He sat in a rocking chair in my living room. In the beginning, it had seemed like a simple arrangement, letting him store some things at my place, but now I realized that there were strings attached. Nelson appeared without warning at my door, ostensibly to drop off another box but in fact to sit around and shoot the breeze. He was lonely. Sometimes I didn't mind the company but I didn't like the presumption, or his proprietary manner when he strode into the living room and went directly to sit in the rocking chair. *His* rocking chair.

"How about some coffee?" he called to me in the kitchen.

Since I was ready for coffee myself, I went ahead and put on the pot. While it brewed I brought out the cups.

"When you gonna get curtains?" he asked. "Jesus, it's like a fish bowl in here."

I didn't answer, though it was true that I was long overdue to do something for these windows. My landlord Mr. Simms had equipped the house with roll-down shades which had an annoying tendency to snap up unexpectedly or refuse to rewind unless you coaxed them *just so*. I'd grown tired of fiddling with them, and left my downstairs windows uncovered during the day. Recently I'd been startled by a face at the window. It scared the hell out of me. A second later, I realized that it was a deer, with its nose almost touching the glass. Then, when I made a movement, I startled *it*. In a blink the deer disappeared, with the suddenness of someone saying *Poof*.

Now I went to the windows and pulled down two shades. Miraculously, they stayed in place on the first try.

"So what's the deal with you, really?" Nelson continued. "A single guy, no relationships. No fucking curtains. If you're not careful people are gonna think you're some kind of loser. Got any sugar?"

I went back to the kitchen and returned a moment later with a paper packet of sugar that had come with a carry-out. "This is all I got. I don't use sugar, so I don't keep it around."

"See what I mean! For God's sake. If it wasn't for my stuff here, this place would be an empty shell."

"Oh, so you're doing *me* a favor," I said. "Glad we got that straight."

Nelson gave me a prim little nod, and smiled.

"You know," I continued, "one of the things that really struck me when I came back to America is the number of storage outlets along the highways. Didn't use to see that. People have so much extra crap that they can't keep it at home. How important can it be?"

"That's not my point. Sure, sometimes less is more. But listen, man—you got too much less. In other ways you don't seem like a social retard. Are you making some kind of statement? You think you're Gandhi?"

"No, it's not a statement."

Nelson stirred his coffee and began to tell me about seeing his daughter over Thanksgiving break, though I didn't follow closely, and mainly heard his words as a wash of sound. I felt an urge to speak about myself, and to ask him what he knew about Amy Rawlings. I wanted to go beyond Mrs. Gordon's gossip. Obviously, there was the question of her husband, too, which I now broached indirectly, interrupting:

"Do you know many people who do meth, Nelson?"

He shrugged. "I see them around. Leo Mitchell, for sure, and some of those other kids working double shifts at Jaycee's or the ethanol plant. They're all ex-students of mine. Teachers don't like to talk about it much because it's sort of a parallel universe, makes the town look bad." He coughed. "You're not going to tell me you're experimenting with that, are you? Gandhi is a tweaker?"

"No, that's not what I meant."

"Good. I wouldn't have been ready for that. Party down with the chemicals you'd use to power a garden tiller. Uh huh."

A shade spun upward—*schtap!* We both jumped. I expected Nelson to make a remark about this fact, but instead he stared out into the grey winter light.

"You know how I feel lately?" he said. "Time is getting away from us. Sometimes when everything is still and quiet, or even when it's not, I find myself *listening* to time passing. Sometimes I hear it *racing* past, whistling in my ears. What are we gonna do?" He gripped his coffee mug, drank with an audible suck, and his eyes darted. "There it went again! Did you hear it?"

☾

"He was fucking this girl at the office—"

(said Amy the next Sunday afternoon in a motel room, after I'd pretended to be surprised when she said that she'd found him one day trying to gas himself in their garage)—"See, that's where Reggie started using meth, at *work*, if you can believe it. He was putting in long hours and it helped him stay sharp. Plus he was fucking this young girl, this little girl with a high voice—you'd think she was fifteen, to hear her talk and to look at her. She was one of his agents. They'd get high together. Reggie says that she was the one that started him on it but there's no reason for me to believe him. He's told so many lies. What does it matter, now? I just thought he was working all the time because I could usually reach him at the office.

"When he was home he was always busy, too, working on spreadsheets and putting Post-its everywhere. That was his favorite thing, sticking up Post-its, and then rearranging them. He covered his computer screen with them. Dumb as I was, I didn't know he was high even then, just goobing around. He didn't smoke crystal at the house. He did it in a little office set up with his little girl. Keeping it restricted to mainly one place was like some bullshit point of honor for him. It meant that he was maintaining, that he was keeping things under control, that he wasn't really addicted—though he told me later that sometimes at the house, he'd use a Post-it as a tooter and take a snort, to tide him over.

"All this time, Reggie was still earning at his job—earning a lot, actually. It's his dad's real estate business but Larry—that's his dad—is semi-retired and Reggie pretty much took over the whole show. He carried the ball. It got to the point where he wasn't sleeping for days at a stretch. He'd come home to me and Ginny and take us out to dinner and he'd be all friendly, really nice, and then he'd go back to the office and work or do God knows what with that girl. They'd go back to their little den with a pipe and put on their fucking moon boots, or however it is they say it. He claims he didn't shoot it.

"This went on for months, maybe more—Reggie can be a very smooth and persuasive person—and I didn't know a damn thing till I found him that day in the garage. It was just by chance that I got there in time. He left a suicide note on the dashboard—he wrote it on a Post-it, actually. Now I haven't told *anybody* this part, Stanley. Of course, the note was short. It said, 'My heart is yours.' What do you think of that?"

There was a catch in her voice and I thought that she might start crying. Yet she seemed to want to tell me these things. I lifted myself up on one elbow, propped on the pillow. I said, "It sounds like he was thinking about you at the end. He cared about you."

Amy turned to me, and I realized that I was wrong; she wasn't on the verge of tears. Her eyes shone with anger. "Sweet, huh?" she said. "That's what I thought, too. But you know what? That note wasn't even for me. It was for his little tweaker girl."

Her voice had become tight; she looked away again.

"How do you know?" I asked.

"I didn't, at first. Oh, Stanley, I was such a sucker. He still wanted to have sex a lot, and I thought it was just me. By then he started having a hard time getting high, and he was using just to maintain. He was paranoid, going off his nut. He was afraid that people were catching on to him and he thought that he was being spied on. He had this crazy idea that me or the police or even his dad Larry had planted microphones in his car, so he cut open the seats and ripped out the upholstery, looking for wires. Later, when I found all that damage inside his car, I thought, what on earth is this? It made no sense at the time. He explained it to me later. Ginny had actually noticed the cuts in the seats before he tried to kill himself, and he'd asked her if she'd seen anybody fooling around with his car. He wanted her to spy on the spies. She didn't mention it to me when it happened. Of course a child couldn't understand what it was about. Poor little Bughouse probably saw lots of things that I didn't see, but it's hard to ask her about that stuff now, you know? Anyway, as for Reggie's *girlfriend*, she had it worse. She tried to stop using—at least she had the guts for that, I'll give her that much credit—but when she did, her body shut down and she could barely get out of bed. She was sleeping something like twenty hours a day. She still lived with her parents—I didn't tell you that part, did I? See what I mean, a *little girl*. Maybe twenty-two years old. But her parents were smarter than I was and they figured that she was suffering from some kind of withdrawal and took her to the hospital. But it was worse than withdrawal. At the hospital the doctors put her directly in the ICU after they checked her heart. Her heart was supposed to have something like seventy-five percent fluid rejection—you know, when the heart pumps, it pushes out what goes in? Turns out, she had less than ten percent. This kid needed a transplant! That's what Reggie was referring to in his note. He'd just gotten the news and what he wrote, he meant *literally*. He was killing himself for romance. He wanted to give her his heart, to be the donor. Extra sweet, huh?"

"Uh, I see."

"Of course he was completely out of his fucking mind, that sort of plan could never work. She tested positive for trace amounts, so she couldn't be a candidate for a heart transplant until she went through rehab and was clean for six months. That's the way it's done. Even when it looks like a person might not survive that long, the doctors say tough shit, because a transplant is a very serious and complicated procedure and they're not going to waste an organ on some dumb addict who is just going to go out and fuck it up again on meth. There are candidates on the waiting list who are more deserving. And when all this happens last spring, I'm thinking: do *I* deserve this? Did *I* ask for this? We had a great life going, we really did."

And now she began to cry, which caught me off guard, and she wouldn't let me take her in my arms. She got out of bed and began to dress. "I don't know what I'm doing here, either. This is the last time we do this, Stanley. Sorry."

It seemed there was nothing else for me to say. But, in the middle of the week, she called me and suggested that we meet again. Sunday afternoons were convenient for her because that was when Reggie was involved with his twelve-step group.

Our motel was the Kingler Motor Inn, which was located near a freeway exit at a middle distance between us, conveniently out of my school district. It had flashing Christmas lights at the entrance and an electric Santa Claus stood in the bushes, loitering like a fat hippie. I don't recall who used the expression first, but we started referring to our rendezvous as "conferences"—as in parent-teacher conferences. The motel had a tiny indoor swimming pool, too, and this time we brought along our bathing suits and, after our conference in the room, we emerged to take a dip and then lie on lounge chairs, gazing out the steamed windows at the never-ending waves of frozen corn stubble which stretched like an ocean as far as the eye could see. We joked that we should call this place Kingler-by-the-Sea, which sounded more exotic. The subject of her husband Reggie didn't come up this time. The owner of the Kingler Motor Inn, a friendly Indian from Madras named Prakesh, brought out a plate of pappadams for us. We bit into the spicy crackers, and agreed that we must do this again, next Sunday.

But the next weekend, no one went anywhere. A winter storm swept across the state, freezing rain, followed by heavy snow, and then the temperature plummeted below zero. Amy called on Saturday night to cancel our conference, a very brief message of less than ten seconds. On Sunday I stayed indoors and surfed the internet, where I found a website for Amy's boutique, Tivoli's. The site had an attractive home page and a flattering photograph of Amy in one corner; but when I clicked the link entitled "About Me," it opened to a page which said *Under Construction.*

School was cancelled for two days, so we had a shortened week leading up to our Christmas vacation. Even after we returned to work, the atmosphere had changed. A new, harsh season had descended. At the end of the school day, after locking up my classroom, I left the building and paused on the front steps to pull on my gloves. The sky was pig-iron grey and threatened more snow. Birds—fat sparrows—perched on the electric wires overhead, motionless. I watched Les the janitor, lowering an icy stiff flag from the pole. The flag resisted his efforts to fold it, and then gave way all at once, popping.

My pupils were happy, though, in a quivering, over-excited state about Christmas. On the last day before the vacation, I followed Mrs. Gordon's instructions and organized a class party. We had games and soft drinks and cake. Ginny Rawlings didn't win any contests but she laughed along with the other children; and when it was finished I helped her pack up Anita the guinea pig, wrapping a towel around the travel cage to keep out the frigid drafts. "We wouldn't want her to get a sore throat," I told her, and Ginny nodded soberly. I was partly kidding but since I was her teacher, she took everything I said very literally. Instead of wearing a stocking cap like the other kids, Ginny pulled on a blue beret. This was surely her mother's touch. Ginny peered into the travel cage, baring her gapped teeth at Anita. It wasn't particularly cute, but it was a pretty successful attempt to look rodentlike. "So what do you and Anita have planned for Christmas?" I asked.

"Anita will stay with my grandma," she said. "I'll be with Mom and Dad."

"That's nice," I said, smiling, and watched her leave with her arms full. Once she was out of sight, I let out a deep breath, and began to straighten the room. After all the noise and high voices, the silence was welcome. I paused to look out the window through a snaggle of overhanging icicles. The afternoon light was retreating, the snow giving it up. Light was drawn toward the lip of the horizon, roseate. Somewhere out there, beneath the snow, was a baseball field.

"Don't be a fool," I said aloud. "There's a kid. What the hell are you thinking, Stanley?"

☾

"You're not going to be lonely?" my mother asked on the telephone.

She was jetting off to Catalina Island with Archie for the holiday. They'd made their arrangements long ago.

"No, I'll be fine."

"Speck, there's not much room in our cabin in Wisconsin," my brother Riley said, "but we could squeeze you in with the boys. We'll let you dress up as Santa."

"Thanks, but I have other plans," I lied.

On Christmas Eve I did some last-minute shopping for myself at Leroy's Supermarket. A year ago I'd spent the holiday with Delphine in Paris, eating capon and oysters, totally unaware of the existence of Legion and the future that awaited me. It was a weird thought. I moved through the fresh produce section: a pyramid of waxy apples, a pile of potatoes and heads of iceberg lettuce. There were some dried-out looking oranges and shipped-in giant strawberries. I was hesitating in front of them, wondering if they had any taste, when I saw Jim and Christine Snow, amusing themselves at the end of the aisle.

Jim picked up a head of lettuce. "Catch," he said, and lobbed it to Christine. She caught it awkwardly against her stomach and walked over and put it back. She looked over her shoulder toward the checkout. "Stop it. You're gonna get us in trouble." Jim picked up an apple, and feigned biting it. "Stop!" Christine said.

Presently a squat little woman arrived from the other direction, pushing a trolley. Her blond ringlets, her resemblance to Christine, were striking. She was a widow, Mrs. Gordon had told me. Her husband had farmed and when that became too unprofitable, he'd worked construction, including pouring the concrete for the Double Dee hog barns. He'd died when his pick-up truck hit a snow plow head-on, two winters ago. "What're you doing?" Mrs. Snow asked. "Where's Billy? I thought he was with you."

"He must be up front," said Christine.

They moved toward the checkout and, when I picked up a container of strawberries and turned to continue my shopping, I was startled to see Billy, peering around the frozen foods aisle, watching the same scene—or, more exactly, watching me watch them. He looked up at me with deep blue eyes. Curls of straw-colored hair escaped from his stocking cap. I thought he was going to say something, and I remembered that day by the river, when he'd spied me spying on them. Now I wondered, not for the first time: had he told the others? Did they know that I watched them? But what was I looking for? These children unintentionally had a way of making you question *yourself.*

Now I said, "Hello, Billy. Excited about Christmas?"

When I said his name, he gave a barely perceptible nod, and then, without a word, he hurried past me to join his family.

☾

ON CHRISTMAS Day I lazed around, enjoying a certain sweet melancholy that comes from spending a holiday alone. In the afternoon I put on several layers of clothing and zipped up my coat and took a long hike across fields of snow and brittle dead weeds. Reaching a creek that led toward the river, I stepped onto black ice, where powdered snow blew in wisps across its surface. I walked down the creek, taking advantage of the open path, my boots squeaking on the cold slick finish. It was like following an enameled alley, a black passage etched into the landscape, curling and winding like a child's cursive writing. I remembered how, when I'd arrived at this place in the summer, gooseberry bushes had clung to the banks and the bramble was almost impenetrable. It had hummed with heat and sleeping birds. Now, with the descent of winter, the page was fresh again.

On my way back to the house I passed through the orchard, where I approached the bell on the post. I pulled the chain. There was a squeak—then nothing. My heart was full of a longing that I didn't know where to put.

☾

"GOD, I just need to relax for a minute," Amy said, running her hands through her hair as she sat up very straight in her chair. She'd changed our meeting place from the Kingler Motor Inn to a cinnamon-smelling tearoom in West Des Moines. I'd had trouble finding the place, but even so, she arrived after me. "At least Christmas is over. Turkey with Reggie's parents, now *that's* a scene, buddy. Reggie's on a special diet with vitamin supplements and that's all his mother talks about. We make sure he has glucosamine and chondroitin. He's working on the twelve steps; he gets counseling. We get counseling together, too. But the thing is, Stanley, I shouldn't be doing what I've been doing with you to get over the counseling. That's what it comes down to. But that's not right, is it?"

"Is that how you see it?"

"Listen to me, Stanley. In counseling it's all about overcoming addiction. They talk like it's the only subject in the whole freaking world. Let's just say I'm a little saturated on that one, okay?" She brought her cup to her lips and took a slow sip. "With Reggie's friends and family, I can't be honest like this or they get alarmed. It's like proof that I'm not supportive enough or I've enabled him. *I'm not worthy.* That's how they see it and it makes me so angry. It's not even about Reggie, it's about *them.* Which is stupid because the point is, *people* don't matter. What matters to Reggie is the meth. That's what captured his heart, what made him want to give it away. Reggie actually said that in counseling, it's not my interpretation. He said using meth was like falling in love, like the first real girlfriend, the one you never forget, but *better.*"

While she was telling me this, a number of images went through my mind from some snooping I'd done. The day after Christmas I'd felt very restless, and after admitting to myself that sometimes I didn't even *like* Amy Rawlings that much, let alone love her, I'd gotten into my Pontiac and driven to a home improvement store in Des Moines where I tried to divert my brain (because I couldn't stop thinking about her! that was the insane part!) with the project of getting curtain accessories for the meth house. I squeezed through the post-Christmas crowds and bought a kit of rings and brackets and oak ball finials, and some precut wooden rods as thick as baseball bats. The curtains I could pick out later, when the shopping was less congested.

Then, driving through a residential neighborhood on my way out of town, still thinking about her (what was wrong with me? why couldn't I stick a finger in my brain and claw out this image of her?), I had a surprise. In the front yard of a house, planted on a crust of snow, was a sign for Rawlings Realtors. It had a photo and a caption: *Call Reggie 572-7545.* I hit the brakes, shifted the car to reverse, and backed up. I got out of the car.

The face smiled at me. A dark-haired guy in a tie, reasonably handsome. A dusky look around the eyes. Confident.

So there you are, I thought. It gave me an odd feeling.

I got back in my car and drove on, and now it occurred to me to go and see where Reggie and Amy lived. Why not? I'd already intruded in their lives in more important ways. Out of curiosity I'd already looked at Ginny's information file and checked where she lived in Legion. Her grandmother's place was a neat little square house with ornamental shrubs and bird feeders. I hadn't seen Colleen, not yet; Amy had told me that she was a nurse on early retirement. She'd injured her back at work, where she'd had to move too many fat patients in their beds. "It pained her so, but she kept doing it because she thought it was her duty. Toward the end it really messed her up. She's partially disabled. Having Ginny around is good for her spirits," Amy had said.

Now I pulled my Pontiac into a convenience store on Army Post Road, checked the phone book, and asked for directions. Along the way, I saw other For Sale signs for Rawlings Realtors, with the same photo of Reggie. It felt as if Reggie were watching me, each step of the way. When I passed Ingersoll and then Grand Avenue and reached .the correct address, Amy's situation became much clearer.

"Jesus," I said.

It was a very attractive cedar-shingled house with a land-scaped front yard, and a large stone chimney climbing up one side. Black branches from enormous old trees in the back-yard rose above the roof. It would be an exaggeration to call it a mansion. Amy and Reggie's home wasn't oversized and glassy like my brother Riley's new construction. But its restraint was an expression of taste, of self-assurance. Above all, of well-to-do respectability. All the houses on this block looked this way.

I put the car in gear and moved on, taking a slow tour of the neighborhood, which offered more of the same, as well as a few places that could be described as mansions, with a Christmas wreath on each pillar, visible through the security fencing. *So this was Amy's life now . . .*

"Now I'm going to tell you something really sick," she said to me across the table at the tearoom.

"Yes?"

"This happened just a few days ago, right before Christmas Eve. Reggie made a list of people that he's harmed, and he wants to make amends to them. It's one of his steps. Of course I'm on the list, and so is Sheila. I got roped in—"

"Sheila?"

"His girlfriend at work. Or ex-girlfriend. The one he used to get high with. I've told you about her."

"Oh, yeah. Right."

"I got roped in to a meeting where I had to see her. I don't know what I was thinking but sometimes you say yes to something because you think it's going to help somebody and then it turns out wrong, totally weird. You see, Sheila's parents had contacted Reggie, because she wanted to see him, but that was out of the question, for a bunch of reasons, the most obvious one being me. But then in counseling he comes up with another scenario, where he goes to see her and *I come along,* and he makes a little speech about how he's clean now and committed to our marriage and he wants to declare in front of both of us that he intends to repair to the best of his abilities the damage he's done. Idiot that I am, I went along with this.

"We go to see Sheila. She's still living with her parents in a house as big as a shoebox. I knew it was a mistake the minute we walked in, but by then it's too late, and we're standing there in the living room with Sheila's mother staring at us, sort of alarmed but glad to see us, too, I could tell, while the father goes down the hall to get Sheila out of her room. The TV is playing loud, it's going all the while this is happening, and the Christmas tree is like *sagging* from too many decorations and all this sad tinsel. *Finally* Sheila comes out in her bathrobe and slowly looks at us and nods a little but she doesn't even say hello. She looked terrible. I'd only seen her once before, at a company picnic when she seemed like a kid in her halter top, but now she looked all skaggy and needed to wash her hair. It's not just that she'd aged, though there was that, too. She's stopped using meth longer than Reggie but in addition to her heart condition that makes her mainly an invalid, it takes only two seconds to see that she's depressed. That's obvious as can be.

"Her parents were slow to leave the room, like they're afraid for her to be out of their sight, and then Reggie makes his speech while the TV is still going. I wanted to run out to the car but I stick it out, and I start to have the impression that Sheila's not really listening to him, or catching half of what he says. That's her business, but it makes me sort of mad, too. And there's something else about her face. I don't know how to say it, but it's kind of swollen and baggy at the same time, like she's wearing a face that's one size too big? This isn't nice, but I think to myself: it's not just depression, she looks retarded.

"And then she looks right back at me, really spooky—it's like she can read my mind. She interrupts Reggie. 'Don't go so fast, I can't follow. My brain is broke.' Those were her exact words. *My brain is broke.* And that was awful, Stanley. Beyond words. There's both her heart and mind, all shot to hell. We got out of there and we both cried in the car afterward, but I was still mad at Reggie. He's the lucky one. What does that little girl have left? You tell me. Her soul?"

☾

"And what are your resolutions for the New Year?" Mrs. Gordon asked in the teachers' lounge, her cheerful face blocking out all light as I poured myself a cup of tepid coffee.

Spend less time talking to you?

I didn't say this, but simply shrugged and smiled.

"Did you get my messages?" asked Chadwick, dipping one of last year's gingersnaps into his cup.

"Oh, yeah. Sorry I didn't get back to you. I wasn't around."

Over the break, Chadwick had left messages on my voice mail, inviting me to join him on New Year's Eve at the New Tabernacle. It would be a Celebration of Fellowship. As it happened, I ended up spending New Year's Eve at a Greek steak house twenty miles down the road where, mercifully, there was no loud music or forced cheer, just a satisfying dinner. When I came home that night, my voice mail announced a new message. It wouldn't be Amy, I knew. (She had a commitment to attend a special New Year's Eve party with members of Reggie's twelve-step program . . . what fun!) Geez, Chadwick, I thought as I pushed the button. Why can't you lay off?

"Happy New Year, Stanley! Where are you? You should be here with us. *Whoooooo!*"

At first I didn't even recognize the voice. There were shouts and background music, and it sounded like quite a party. I replayed the message, and realized that it was Beverly.

"Hey Binky," I said, and fell into bed.

Back in my classroom, the New Year meant a chance for kids to flaunt their recently acquired holiday spoils. That first day I confiscated three Game Boys that pupils couldn't resist playing with during lessons. Brain Rush had a solar-powered calculator, which shouldn't have been objectionable, but it got confiscated, too, because he wouldn't shut up talking about it. Ginny Rawlings had a sleek new leather book bag (*Now*, I thought, *if you would only read a book!*), while Callie Graham offered another kind of distraction: she sported eyeliner and high black patent-leather boots, Christmas presents that made her look like some kind of kiddie dominatrix. (Jesus, what were her parents thinking?) And, worst of all, Curtis Teas, for some inexplicable reason, kept a spare battery for his new MP3 player in his *mouth*. At first I thought he was rolling around a piece of hard candy, and I told him to spit it out. But it was a battery. How many days had he been doing this? I wondered if it had pacified him for his vacation: the slow poisoning of Christmas detritus. It became a topic in our science class. "Okay, everybody," I announced, "write this down: *do not suck on batteries*. Got that? It's unhealthy."

My pupils were also supposed to turn in a 200-word essay, composed over the holidays, on any subject of their choosing. It wasn't a serious assignment, but a ploy to keep them from disconnecting totally from school during the break. Ginny Rawlings wrote:

> There was a weener dog named Jerry driving his car to Calfornia and there was a ~~dog~~ cat named penny at the gas station for nachos. They went so fast and it was funny no one is there. They push the horn they saw mountains. an mountains and mountains. And mountains and mountains and mountains and mountains and mountains and mountains and mountains and mountains and mountains and mountains and mountains and mountains and mountains and mountains and mountains and mountains and mountains and mountains and mountains and mountains

mountains mountains mountains mountains mountains
mountains mountains mountains mountains mountains
mountains mountains mountains mountains mountains
mountains mountains mountains mountains mountains
mountains mountains mountains mountains mountains
mountains mountains mountains mountains mountains
mountains mountains mountains mountains mountains
mountains mountains mountains mountains mountains
mountains mountains mountains mountains mountains
mountains mountains mountains mountains mountains
mountains mountains mountains mountains mountains
mountains mountains mountains mountains mountains
mountains mountains mountains mountains mountains
mountains mountains mountains mountains mountains
mountains mountains mountains mountains mountains
mountains mountains mountains mountains mountains
mountains mountains mountains mountains mountains

7

I got a cat. On a murky February morning, a smoky grey tom greeted me at my back door, mewing, begging. He was young, very thin, even starving in appearance. I had no idea where he came from and gave him some milk while I went back inside and shaved.

Of course, this was only the beginning. The cat hung around the back steps and soon I let him in and he took up residence. I started calling him Wally. It wasn't a name I was particularly fond of, but it seemed to fit. Mr. Worthington's first name was Walter. Behind his back, sometimes teachers referred to him as Wally.

"Go eat a mouse, Wally. It's on the house."

He padded cautiously from room to room, exploring. He was bizarrely elastic. When Wally went around a corner he didn't walk around it, he *bent* around it. "Relax," I told him. "You're in civilization now. Just don't shit anywhere."

He looked up at me with bulging yellow eyes and let out a screaky meow. He sounded as if he'd swallowed a burr.

The first few days I fed him scrambled egg, but soon took to buying canned cat food, a foul-smelling, glaucous, liver-based glop which I spooned into a bowl and lowered to the linoleum. Wally consumed it like a demon—he gobbled and sucked and suddenly it was gone—then he sauntered away across the kitchen, swaying, his sides visibly distended.

One Saturday morning, after stocking up on cat food at Leroy's Supermarket, I was putting bags in the trunk of my car when a voice called to me.

"How's that Pontiac running? You want a dog?"

I turned around and faced Roy Heffernan. He'd caught me by surprise and it took me several seconds to recognize him.

"The car is fine, thanks."

"I've had seven puppies to get rid of and I'm down to my last two. Don't want to give them the hammer. You want a dog? It's weaned."

"No thanks. I got a cat."

"So? You can have a cat and a dog."

He kept talking, trying to persuade me. In other circumstances I would've invented an excuse and got in my car, but Roy Heffernan looked haggard. It wasn't only that he was poorly shaven; he seemed to have aged since I'd last seen him. It was cold standing in the street, so I invited him for a cup of coffee at the diner on the corner of Legion's town square.

The place was called Dwight's. I didn't go to Dwight's often because the owner was a fervent Bernie booster who'd tried to recruit me to coach the high school baseball team. Word had got round town that I used to play. No thank you, I'd told him, knowing the many extra hours, travel and lost weekends that went along with coaching. Dwight had persisted with me in a badgering manner that implied that I was lacking in loyalty, that I didn't give a damn about the local team. This was true, too—but a person couldn't come out and say so, not in Dwight's Diner.

This morning I waved at Dwight as we entered and he glowered at me from behind the grill. Roy and I sat in a booth and a teenaged waitress with a nose piercing—name-tag "Gemmi"—filled our mugs. Roy asked Gemmi for a slice of sour cream raisin pie. I sipped my coffee, and asked him if it had been a difficult winter at his farm.

"Oh, I'm okay, but I just spent a few days at a neighbor's who needed some help. You know the Van Dykes? What a mess. They're just a couple of miles southwest of me, near the township line road?"

I shook my head.

"They got hit by TGE," he said.

"What's that?"

"You know. Like flu. Gastroenteritis."

"That'll usually pass in a day or two."

Roy peered at me over his cup, grinning. Then his grin broadened. "You're not kidding, are you?" He burst out laughing, and slapped the table. Gemmi came over with the pie and put it down in front of him and, instead of leaving, stood by to learn what was so funny. Roy leaned back and guffawed in my face, showing me the shiny fillings in his teeth. "You're too much," he said. "A guy like you, teaching our kids!"

It's no pleasure to be laughed at, but I didn't know how to answer him. One of my elbows on the table felt the grit of salt from a previous customer. "What?" I asked, rubbing my arm. "What did I say?"

"I'm not talking about *people*," he told me. "TGE is for hogs. And it's no joke, mister, that's not what I'm saying. Vomiting and diarrhea, and you have to heat the building up to eighty degrees, otherwise the hogs get chilled and die. Especially the nursing pigs. They can't take the dehydration. We give them a strawberry milkshake drink for treatment. That's about all you can do. You've never seen such diarrhea! It has a special smell of its own. It'll shoot out three feet behind."

He spread his arms in an imaginary shitty arc.

Gemmi snorted, and walked away.

"Wow," I said. "Was this at the Double Dee?"

"No, they avoid it. It's my neighbor, I'm telling you, Carl Van Dyke. You've probably seen his son Deacon around town."

Now I recalled—the big kid, the football player. He drove a four-by-four with a faulty muffler that roared like a teenage mating call.

"Poor Carl, he doesn't know what he'll do next. He's lost most of his stock. We spent part of this morning grinding up dead pigs to feed them to the sows. It works like a vaccination. Hogs are fragile creatures. That's why I've always preferred beef, personally. Ever since I was a kid."

He took a forkful of pie.

"How does the Double Dee avoid it?" I asked.

"Oh, they use farrowing crates, that sort of thing. It's cleaner, in its way, the hogs get fewer infections. But the hog can't move or even turn around, it just shits between the slats. There's no straw and it's pretty miserable. Their leg bones get fragile and the bones fracture easy from lack of use. Still, hygiene is what everybody wants nowadays, and damn the rest."

"It's a good thing there are people like you and Van Dyke," I told him. "People who aren't doing it the Double Dee way."

This remark was intended to be friendly. It was my stab at having a conversation about farming in Dwight's Diner. But the words seemed to irritate him. Roy took a big swallow.

"You don't say? Well, Carl's in big trouble, and frankly his boy might be better off working for the Double Dee. He'd get a regular shift and maybe some insurance if he went up the ladder. He could sleep nights and get away when he has a vacation. And he might pay off his house instead of losing it."

"Would you work for them?" I asked.

He grimaced.

"That's different, I'm almost retired. Sure, I'd rather work for myself. But it's not so that town people can feel superior to the ag business. I'm nobody's pet rustic."

Obviously this wasn't a good subject, and I regretted trying to be friendly in the first place. Roy Heffernan was a hardened man. It took more than "friendly" to impress him. I reached in my pocket for my money—our conversation had pretty much run its course—when, to my surprise, Roy began to speak quickly, in nervous rushes, as if he didn't want to let me get away. It was like the pitch he'd given me earlier about the dogs, where I'd vaguely sensed that we weren't really talking about dogs, or not *only* about them, but of some larger, more important subject. Roy Heffernan was hungry for attention. Even *my* attention. It was strange. I'd replaced his wife at school and now, for a brief time on a lonely Saturday morning,

I was replacing her for conversation. His old support was gone and he was grabbing at anyone.

I sat back in the booth, pausing with the money in my hand. "How are your children, Roy? What do they do?"

He didn't seem to mind the question. His children were grown up, he explained. His daughter was married and lived out of state, and his son was a graduate student in chemical engineering. "He's a smart fella but he just plans to stay in school forever. There's no way he's coming back here. My kids don't want much to do with the farm. I'm all for being sustainable but it takes *people*. People on the ground."

"When do you think you'll retire?"

He shrugged. "And do what?"

"Well, something more fun than grinding your neighbor's pigs."

"Fun, huh?" He slid his tongue across the front of his teeth. "That's not the point, is it?" He pushed aside his pie plate. "It's a peculiar thing. Everybody talks about 'saving the family farm.' It's always the same tune. The same song and dance. Even the Double Dee advertises that way, though you'd be an idiot to believe them. But I feel like saying, 'I've *done* it, damn you. I've outsmarted you all. I've still got my farm. But where's the family?'"

I fingered my coffee cup, not knowing what to say.

"Time for me to get a move on," he said. "Got stuff to do."

❦

AFTER THIS cheerful conversation with Roy Heffernan, I went home and put away the groceries, and felt the need to do something constructive, so I pulled out the curtain kit that I'd bought after Christmas. I still hadn't got round to assembling it. I emptied out the kit bag and the contents made quite a clatter: brackets and rings, and a wooden ball finial rumbled and rolled across the floor. Wally scooted after it, his feet skittering under him in his haste. I picked up a curtain rod and swung it like a bat, twenty, thirty times. My shoulders got nice and loose, the swings became smooth, and I started thinking: *Don't call her, Stanley. Don't do it. It's her turn now.*

I'd seen Amy a few more times since the New Year. Once we met at Kingler-by-the-Sea and had gone straight to bed. It was very good. Another time we quarreled and by the end of the meeting had agreed to cut out seeing each other, because no good could come of our encounters. Two weeks later we'd met yet again.

I'd come to recognize in Amy a restless vanity that I'd always possessed myself. Maybe that was what we really shared. It wasn't a good quality but it wasn't the sort of thing you could easily control: a nagging sense that your real life wasn't the one you were living but was waiting for you somewhere else; your real life hadn't quite begun yet. This real life, needless to say, was better, more intense and beautiful than what you lived now. What other people saw of you and thought was your life—oh, that was merely a temporary arrangement. A passing distraction. Not truly *you.*

Recently I'd annoyed her by stopping by Tivoli's. I was at the new mall, shopping for a cheap DVD player, and I was curious to see Amy's boutique. I spotted it from afar, recognizing the red-lettered sign, the same as the logo on her website. When I walked in, she looked very surprised.

"Hey there!" I said. "How's business?"

After the initial jolt, she quickly recovered. Amy shrugged. She stood behind the counter, holding a carry-out coffee cup from which she took a sip, but the cup seemed to be empty, because she tilted it very far. Then she said, "Not so great, actually. Business could be better."

"Well, maybe it's the slow season," I said. "It'll improve."

"Maybe."

There was a silence during which I was struck by the brightness of the shop lights, and the reflections of the mirrors behind her. She wore a cream cashmere sweater, and the slender strap of a dark blue brassiere was visible on one shoulder. "I haven't heard from you for a while. Is everything all right?"

"Busy," she said. "Busy."

Suddenly she leaned away as if crowded by my presence.

"Stanley, please don't stand here like that. Could you go over there and act like a customer? We're being watched."

"Watched?"

"Just do as I say. I can explain later."

So I moved away from the counter and pretended to inspect some belts and other leather goods, and then some cashmere sweaters like the one she was wearing, before reaching into a rack and pulling out a top. It was an attractive silver, partly silk, and it looked like Amy's size. I returned to the register.

"I like this one, but how much is it? It doesn't seem to have a price tag."

"I haven't got round to marking everything. Eighty dollars. Will that be cash or credit?"

Expensive, yes. But, since she'd said that business was slow, I reached for my wallet. While she rang it up, we spoke in low tones and arranged to meet the following Sunday afternoon at Kingler-by-the-Sea.

This time, she didn't cancel on me, but she was late to arrive at the motel and one of the first things she said was, "We're not going to have sex. If you're really my friend, we don't have to do that." Instead, she wanted to go to the fitness center. She'd brought along a gym bag with shorts and shoes. I was irritated. If she'd told me in advance, I would've at least brought my gear, too; but, in the end, it didn't matter, since the "fitness center" at the Kingler Motor Inn amounted to a small windowless room with a rickety step machine and a few adjustable dumbbells. We spent most of our time standing around and talking. Amy bobbed up and down on the machine, which squeaked terribly, while I did a few curls with the dumbbells, flat-footed in my swimming trunks and socks. After a few minutes, she'd stop and we'd discuss what was going on.

"What did you mean the other night when you said that we were being watched?" I asked.

"Well not you, particularly—it's me and my store. See, Reggie's family handles lots of the commercial leases at the mall, and there's a girl who runs the cell phone counter, right across from Tivoli's, you probably don't even remember. She's *always* there and her family is friends with Reggie's family. Reggie's family set up their business. She's bored and notices my every move, I swear. She's got nothing else to do. You should've let me know that you were coming, Stanley. Or, frankly, you shouldn't have come. It's not a place for us. I'd assumed that you understood that."

"Sorry. I didn't think it through."

She resumed her efforts on the step machine, pitching back and forth like someone standing on the deck of a ship in rough seas, before stopping a short time later, when I'd asked her above the noise, "You're coming to the next conference, aren't you?" I was referring to the real parent-teacher conferences at school, not one of our Sunday afternoon sessions.

"Sure, got it marked on the calendar. You know, Ginny's been through so many disruptions this past year. She deserves better. Colleen deserves better, too. I have to look out for everybody. I don't want Ginny to feel about Reggie the way I felt about my father. We can't get around that."

She went on to explain that when she was a child, her father had left her mother for a girl fresh out of high school, who, it emerged shortly afterward, was pregnant. "They must've been doing it together when she was still a minor—he could've gotten in *big* trouble. Instead they got married and moved to Indianapolis, till he left her for a woman with big fake ones." She held out her hands in front of her. "You men really disgust me sometimes." The machine trembled, its springs went *screak-screak-screak*. She paused again. "Of course, Colleen was humiliated. But she picked up the pieces and kept going. She gets mad if I even try to talk about it. When I was out of the house she married again, a guy called Dutch, who seemed okay at first, he was nice to her, but then he got really sick with colon cancer and Colleen had to take care of him till he died. That was no picnic. It's a good thing we have Ginny!"

After we left the fitness center, Amy ran herself a bath back in the room and our conversation continued while she was in the tub. I put down the toilet lid and sat beside her as she enthused, "I'm getting in a new line of leather goods at Tivoli's. I'm really excited about it. I got a great supplier, this girl I went to college with in Milwaukee. The timing couldn't be better." Hot water sloshed as she soaped her shoulders. A bubble shone blue on her neck. I smelled the rising musk of the water. "Milwaukee?" I asked. "Didn't you tell me you went to school in the East?"

"That's east of here, isn't it? You know, Ginny seems to like you. She told me you're not 'unreal.' That's the expression that's going round now. Anything bad is 'unreal.' It's one of her favorite words. You must be a good teacher."

Amy and I really needed to take time, in an appropriate setting, to talk about Ginny's poor performance. "You're not going to like her next report card," I said. "Your conference is for the Thursday night slot, I think."

With a squeak and a splash she suddenly stood up, water streaming away, beading on her skin. Amy had smallish breasts but very large nipples, which were now erect.

"I'll be there, Mr. Mercer. Stop staring and hand me a towel, will you?"

&

"So what do you think I should do?" I asked Nelson. He'd arrived while I was reading the instructions for my curtain kit, and now he sat in his rocking chair. I'd told him only a fraction of what had happened, and I mentioned no names. Just enough to let him know the circumstances.

"This mom you've been schtoinking," he said, "her kid's in your class, is that what you're saying?"

"Yeah."

"And the kid doesn't know about this?"

"No. Of course not."

"Then quit while you're ahead. Frankly, Stanley, the parent in me wants to strangle you. My God, what's that?"

Nelson looked past me, where Wally was hiding behind one of my stereo speakers. It was one of his favorite places and he could stay there for long periods. Occasionally his face leered over the top like a gargoyle's.

"That's my cat." I went over and extracted him and dropped him in the middle of the floor, where he stood still and stared up at Nelson. Wally had an unfortunate sideways manner of holding his head, which made his body seem askew, and his whiskers crooked.

"What's his name?" Nelson asked. "Jesus, look at that face. He ain't no glamour puss."

When I told Nelson his name, he roared with laughter, rocking back in the chair. This spooked Wally, who darted out the door. Now I felt more annoyed than the situation warranted, but it seemed excessive, on Nelson's part, to criticize my cat in my own living room. He hadn't been invited here in the first place. Why was he always showing up at my door?

Now he crossed his legs and stretched his arms. "Tell me more," he said, "what's this woman like? What do you think she sees in you?"

"Let's just drop it, Nelson. I shouldn't have brought her up in the first place."

"But you felt the need to. You must be stuck on her. Come on, answer the question. What do you think she sees in you?"

He was silent, still rocking. Waiting.

"I'm not sure. I'm probably a way for her to get back at her husband. It's clear that he hurt her bad, I can see that. But—there's probably more to it. We do each other some good. I mean, if she's only trying to get back at her husband, why choose me? He's supposedly some kind of big shot. There's money in the family and he's probably just a daddy's boy, but still. I'm not a very logical competitor. A guy like me doesn't register in those circles."

"But you don't have to be a big shot," Nelson replied. "In this case it's probably better if you're not. That can be a turn-on for some people. Maybe she gets a charge out of slumming."

I looked at Nelson.

"Well, gee. You're a friend. Thanks. That makes me feel a lot better."

There was a movement in the corner of my vision, and I turned to watch Wally walk mincingly across the living room floor, with a dead mouse in his mouth.

He dropped it.

"That must be for you," I told Nelson. "A present."

But it wasn't quite dead. One foreleg twitched, swam pathetically in the air. You could almost believe that it was waving at us. Wally batted the mouse with his paw, and sent it skidding under the couch.

"Time for me to go," Nelson said.

☾

THE LAST week in February, temperatures rose dramatically, the snow and ice melted—the kids at school were ecstatic, running outside without their coats, losing their wits over a taste of warmth—until a few days later when, just as Mrs. Gordon predicted, the temperature dropped dramatically. It plunged to single digits, froze the fresh mud on the playground to a patch as hard as granite, the bare backside of winter, without even snow to cover it up—a place where children fell and broke their arms.

This second round of parent-teacher conferences started more smoothly than the first time because I didn't have to improvise so much; I was less a novice and knew what to expect. For Amy Rawlings' appointment, I resolved to mince no words. Ginny was doing terrible work. Even casual assignments, like the essay she was supposed to do over the Christmas break, seemed beyond her. In fact, that essay was a perfect example of Ginny: her story of Jerry the wiener dog driving his car to California was pleasant enough, but simply infantile, like her handwriting; more troubling, Jerry and Ginny scarcely got started before they ran out of gas. The endless mountains of the rest of the piece were simply a sorry means to pad the essay out to 200 words. Perversely, I counted the words, and the total came to 198; so, even on that score, she'd got it wrong. Unless—and this would be worse—it wasn't an error in calculation but a sign that she'd given up, so close to the finish. Now that really made me sad. It would be unkind to compare her to a classmate like Lisa Carter, whose typed and spell-checked 200 words on the migration pattern of monarch butterflies was almost perfect; but, nonetheless, something *must* be said.

But where was Amy? The woman who approached my desk at the appointed time was someone I'd never seen before. I had no idea who she was—and then, an instant later, it was obvious. The resemblance around the eyes and cheekbones. It was Amy's mother, Colleen.

"Please sit down," I said, my mind going blank. Colleen moved with slow deliberation and seemed shy when shaking my hand. The hair spray on her dark dyed perm made the top of her head look crisp.

"I'm Mrs. Harrison," she introduced herself, "Ginny Rawlings is my granddaughter. She's been living with me while her folks deal with some health issues." She squared up her knees and sat very straight. "You've spoken to Ginny's mother, right? She told me she came to the first conference. She did come, didn't she?"

"Why, yes."

"Good. Ginny's not making trouble, is she?"

"Why, no."

"Good, then." She shifted in her chair, and for a moment I thought she might get up and leave; but she was merely seeking a better alignment with her seat. I recalled Amy saying something about her mother's back problems.

I began to describe, in careful terms, her granddaughter's performance, and soon she cut in.

"Ginny's a sweetie but she's lazy. I don't know where she gets it from. I'm not lazy. Her mom can't sit still, never could. Her dad has done well enough for himself." With these last words her gaze shifted, and I could tell that she was considering how much to share with me about Reggie Rawlings. Evidently this subject hadn't been rehearsed with her daughter. "Ginny spends way too much time in front of the TV and when I tell her to go out and play and let off steam, she runs over to the neighbors and watches TV there. Those kids are younger than she is but she doesn't mind. Ginny's sort of young for her age, you've probably noticed that. She has some catching up to do."

Colleen Harrison's frankness was a relief and, as we grew more at ease, our conversation was constructive. She was less defensive than Amy would've been. "Tell you one thing, though," Colleen put in, "Ginny is no crybaby, nope. She doesn't have that problem." She stuck her chin out while affirming this, and then tucked it back in when she was finished. It appeared challenging, and then deferential, in one continuous movement. She did this several times during our conference. Colleen's voice reminded me of Amy's but her speech was noticeably slower, colored by a small-town twang, which Amy seemed to have shed.

"I suspect that Ginny will do just fine in her own time," I said, trying to end our meeting on a positive note and feeling, as with no other conference this evening, my own precariousness, my lack of qualification to tell her anything. "We just have to get her to focus." I smiled. "She's with her mother tonight, while you're here?"

I was fishing; it was the first question of this sort that I'd asked. Colleen shook her head.

"No, Ginny's with the neighbors. Her mom's in Santa Fe."

(In my mind, I could hear Amy's voice at the motel, promising me about tonight's conference: *I'll be there, Mr. Mercer.*)

Colleen interpreted my silence as another question, and she cleared her throat and said quickly, "Ginny's dad is seeing a doctor out there, they went together. I'll level with you, Mr. Mercer. Her dad is a good fellow but he got mixed up in some drugs and now he's getting help. He's doing better and they're hoping this doctor will tell him how to keep on the right track. It's a very famous clinic and they've been waiting for months to see him. It's been a bad year for everybody but now things are coming back together."

Colleen licked her lips and seemed nervous about this admission.

"Good," I said. "Hope it goes well, Mrs. Harrison."

After this conversation, and watching Colleen slowly leave my classroom, I decided to wash my hands of Amy Rawlings, once and for all. I'd already known that she was capricious and unreliable. At the beginning of the conference, when Colleen had appeared in her place, I'd assumed that it was more of the same: perhaps something had come up at Tivoli's, and she'd changed her mind about driving down to Legion.

But when Colleen told me that Amy had gone to Santa Fe, the truth was more simple. That day at the motel, she'd lied to my face. This wasn't one of her quirks or inconsistencies. She'd known all along that she was going away, but she'd lacked the honesty to tell me. Of course, Amy didn't *owe* me an explanation. She didn't owe me a damn thing. But still. Still.

That night, when it was very late, I sat down and composed a long bitchy email to Beverly recounting the affair, which ended with the statement, "*I've wasted my time with this woman. We're nothing but just pretending and I don't want to pretend anymore. Aren't I too old for this shit?*"

But, fortunately, I didn't send this message. Already I could imagine Beverly's reply. *"Yes, you are."*

I hit DELETE.

❦

WHAT HAPPENED next was probably inevitable. One afternoon in early March I stopped by Legion's post office where I bumped into Shana Linn, who'd come to retrieve her mail. ("Still got vandals?" I asked. "Less now," she replied. "Maybe we're getting past that, or maybe it's seasonal. We'll see.") I did my errand and left the post office, musing over this conversation and watching my feet as I walked, avoiding patches of slush. A recent snow was melting off. Then, abruptly, I looked up and saw Ginny Rawlings on the sidewalk, facing me. A few steps behind her, Amy.

"Oh, hello," I said.

"Hello." She stepped back, readjusting the strap of her purse. "Oh yes, I remember you. You're Ginny's teacher. Good afternoon, Mr. Mercer."

She held out her hand for me to shake it, while Ginny looked on. Amy's show of surprise, her momentary hesitation about my identity, was pitch-perfect. If it hadn't been, I might've slipped and said something amiss, but she acted so well that it made it easy for me to fall into character. I shook her hand and pursued the charade. "Oh yes, Mrs. Rawlings. And how are you?"

It was ridiculous, but in Ginny's presence, what else should we do? This wasn't the right moment to snub Amy, or to tell her something withering or sarcastic. She smiled pleasantly.

"Fine, fine," Amy said. "Ginny just had her dance lesson."

"That's interesting," I claimed, looking down at Ginny. "I didn't know you danced."

Ginny nodded solemnly.

"Tell him what kind you do," Amy said.

– 128 –

"Modern jazz," said Ginny.

"There's a dance studio just down the street. The classes in this town are pretty basic, but she builds on them. Show Mr. Mercer," Amy said.

Ginny hesitated, looking up and down the sidewalk. I didn't understand at first. I certainly didn't expect Ginny to dance *here*. There was a silence and then a raft of wet snow suddenly slipped from the roof of a nearby church and whooshed to the ground with the weight of wetness. As if that were the cue, Ginny began to dance, a jittery grind, with a frantic childish urgency, like someone with a finger in an electric socket. I laughed out loud; I couldn't help myself, while Amy encouraged her, singing in a tripping soprano:

> *Do the bughouse!*
> *You're the bughouse girl,*
> *Do the bughouse!*
> *It's a bughouse world.*

What struck me most was how Ginny gave herself wholly to the performance. Ginny—my shyest pupil!—making this exhibition on a public street. A part of me resisted, on her behalf; she shouldn't be made into a kind of performing monkey. But this qualm was soon conquered. There was something welcome about this dance, under the bleak March sky. Her mother's snappy lilt was effective (I'd never heard Amy sing before, and she sang well). Soon I was captive, and could only stand and marvel.

Amy stopped singing, and Ginny stopped dancing.

"That was great," I said, clapping.

Amy looked at me with triumph in her eyes. "Time for us to go," she said. "Goodbye, Mr. Mercer." She took Ginny's hand and walked away.

THE BEGINNING of April brought warm breezes and the grass began to turn green, and then heavy rains came for days at a stretch. Children looked with disappointment out the windows, leaving nose imprints on fogged glass.

On a Friday afternoon, after locking up my classroom, I offered Jim and Christine a ride home from school. This probably broke a bunch of rules about insurance and I don't know what else but at that moment it seemed the easy and natural thing to do. The Snows were standing under an overhang with other kids, waiting for their bus. It had been a long time since I'd spoken to either of them. "I'll be driving by your place anyway," I lied. "Why don't you come with me?"

They looked surprised, but they accepted my offer. Christine climbed into the front seat, Jim in back. We eased out of the parking lot as Russell's school bus rolled up to the curb. Soon we were in the country.

"Got any plans for the weekend?" I asked.

"Plans?" Christine said.

I looked out my window at ditches and sodden bean fields. Such a lonely place! A person could go mad. "Oh, I don't know. What does Billy like to do?" I asked.

From the back seat came Jim's voice:

"How do you know Billy?"

There was something defensive in this question. I glanced in the mirror and saw his inquisitive eyes. But I wasn't sure how to answer. Driving down the mudslick road, the image of Billy running by the rabbit cages came to mind. So did the sight of him clinging to the tree. But neither of these seemed appropriate, now. I couldn't make these images say anything that came to good.

"I saw him with your mom at the supermarket. You were all there, shopping."

He made no reply, and now my Pontiac approached the lane to their house, and I put the car in low gear.

"Careful how you turn around," said Christine. "When you leave, go straight back in your tracks."

We chugged past the rabbit cages. I strained to see if there were any rabbits inside, but it was impossible to tell. For some reason I wanted very much for the rabbits to be there. The dark line of cages slipped out of sight.

"You kids still keep rabbits?" I asked.

"A few," said Jim.

Bent daffodils surrounded the porch steps, giving an appearance both unruly and friendly. The car slowed to a stop. Christine and Jim opened their doors; they climbed out, cool air swished in. Jim's door chunked closed, while Christine stood on the wet grass and leaned into the front seat. She peered at me, a pale face.

"Is there something we can do for you?"

8

In my mailbox on Saturday, I found a creamy envelope of high-quality paper. Inside, a printed card.

Ruth Mercer and Archie Morel
have the pleasure to invite you
to their wedding at Carson Civic Center
on Saturday, May 14 at 3:30 P.M.

On the back of the invitation was a hand-written message from my mother, about meeting for dinner at Bunty's Showplace, and an allusion to plans for a honeymoon in Mexico.

Well. So it was official. She was making it Dead Serious. Standing in the muddy road by my mailbox, I reread the card and then stuffed it in my coat and walked back to the house. I punched out my mother's telephone number, intending to offer my congratulations. "Yes?" said a man's voice.

I still wasn't accustomed to Archie answering her phone. But maybe he'd moved in by now.

"Hi, this is Stanley. I just wanted to call to congratulate you both."

"Why, thank you! Ruth isn't in right now. She'll be back later. I've got my ingredients all laid out on the cutting board and I'm gonna make her a stir-fry!"

"Well—good for you."

"You're coming for the ceremony, aren't you?" he asked. "Am I finally going to meet the famous Stanley?"

From someone else, "the famous Stanley" might've sounded sarcastic, but I don't think it was, coming from Archie. He was just trying to connect.

"Sure, I'll be there," I told him. "It's not easy to catch you two, you know. You seem to travel a lot."

"I'm a frequent flyer—the more you do, the more you can do," he said. "Neither of us have been to Cancún, so what the hey? Your mother is quite the little gal. We'll get guava oils," he purred.

I had no intention of asking what these were for, so I changed the subject by inquiring if he'd seen my brother Riley lately.

"Oh yes, the whole crew stopped by last weekend. The boys had their Easter shoes. Serena looks big as Santa. The baby's almost due, you know. They—"

While he was speaking, I saw, through my front windows, a green minivan pull into my driveway. I experienced a sinking feeling as I recognized Amy.

"Sorry," I interrupted Archie. "Gotta go."

I moved away from the window and retreated to the kitchen and, when I heard the knock on the front door, I considered ignoring it. Why answer? Why did she come all the way to my place? She hadn't been here since our first night together. But I was curious and, after pacing around the table, I grabbed some sunflower seeds from a bowl and answered the door, adopting a casual air.

"Hey. What's going on?"

I brought a seed to my teeth, and split it.

"Sorry to bother you, Stanley, but I'm in a terrible jam. You have to help me."

She was obviously flustered, her tone was distressed. And, though I was sorry to see her, at the same time I could've reached out and taken her shoulders, brought her close. I wanted to. But I didn't.

"What's the matter?"

She didn't blink. "Could you keep an eye on Ginny for me?"

I moved a seed around on my tongue. "Gee, I don't know. When? What for?"

"Oh, for God's sake, Stanley, I'll explain later. I don't have time."

And then, looking over Amy's shoulder, I noticed that Ginny was sitting in the front seat of the minivan. She waved shyly.

"You mean *now?*" I asked. "Oh come on. You're joking, right? You want me to be your *babysitter?*"

"Do this for me, Stanley. It's an emergency. See, Colleen organized a luncheon today at her place with her old friends from her job at the clinic—she's planned it for like 200 years in advance—and I told her that I could take Ginny for the whole Saturday. But now something has come up. There's trouble at Tivoli's. I can explain later, once I know more myself. Reggie is like, two hours away, he's in the middle of stuff, and there's no one else in Legion I can turn to. I don't want to spoil Colleen's party. Please? I'm asking as a friend."

God knows, this wasn't how I intended to spend my Saturday. Why was I having this conversation? "But *here?* What do we tell Ginny?"

"Oh, that's not a problem. You're her teacher. We'll say it's for tutoring. Jesus Christ, Stanley, there's no reason to make this complicated. All I'm asking is for you to spend a few hours with her. Go over her math or something. You do it all the time. It's not rocket science. I'll never ask you another favor, I swear."

A rushing in my ears. *Hell no! Hell no!*

And then, wordlessly, I nodded. Telling myself that I would do this for Colleen—but knowing, at the same time, that though I found Amy unreasonable, impossible, obnoxious (this was the idiotic part!)—I still wanted her to like me.

Amy spun around and ran back to the minivan. As I watched her open the passenger door and tell Ginny to come in the house, I thought: You ought to be avoided at all costs. But here I am, mixed up in your mixed-up life.

"Well, well," I told Ginny, stepping back to let her enter. "How are you today?"

She gave a nervous giggle but didn't answer. Part of her reaction, no doubt, was seeing her teacher in old jeans and a ragged sweat shirt, unshaven on a Saturday and looking seedy. But she didn't seem intimidated or reluctant to come in my house. After all, I was a familiar person that she saw every day. Maybe she was curious, too. Entering her teacher's house was like turning over a rock to see what was underneath.

On the other hand, once Amy had zoomed away and we settled in, Ginny's curiosity was quickly satisfied. I invited her to watch TV and she nodded and sat primly on the couch and let me turn on the set for her. I went to the refrigerator to see if there was any orange juice left. There wasn't. I rooted around, looking for something appropriate to offer her, but it was bad timing; I'd intended to do my shopping at Leroy's later in the day and, for the moment, was caught short on provisions. When I returned to the living room, Ginny stood next to the TV, pressing the channel-changer button on the remote control and watching the stations flick by, while her other hand rested on top of the set, as if to reassure it.

"You don't have cable?" she asked incredulously. "Even Grandma has cable."

"No, sorry, I don't. Are you hungry, Ginny? I got smoked oysters in a can."

She stared back at me, and it was slightly unnerving, for her *lack* of reaction. I could've been speaking in a foreign language, or reached up and unscrewed my head and placed it atop the TV and continued the conversation: it would've been equally fantastic, in any case. She leaned forward slightly, blinking—but didn't answer. I retreated to the kitchen (why was I letting myself be bullied?) and came back, extending a bowl. "How about some sunflower seeds?"

She pursed her lips. (At least, this time, she acknowledged me.) "They look hard," she said.

Now it was my turn to be slow, because it took me several seconds to realize that she'd never eaten a sunflower seed before. This surprised me. "Well, that's the shell, but it's no problem. You just bite down, like this . . . see? And you take out the good part . . . see? Once I get started, I can't stop. I can eat them all day."

She nodded, as if I'd just confirmed that I was The Most Boring Man in the Universe. I was beginning to feel exasperated. At school, I had a script, and the kids generally followed it. I bossed the herd. But, one-on-one was different. I didn't like it at all. She took some seeds but did nothing with them, looking away, and began to kick her feet on the side of the couch, not deigning to speak.

"Don't do that," I said, and she stopped kicking for a moment; but a short time later, when I mentioned the fruit trees in bloom in the orchard, she started kicking again. Now I was acutely conscious of how much my authority depended on the school setting, and not on me, personally. Ginny was not such a meek creature, in truth. She could be a little snot who got on my nerves.

Any idea of drilling Ginny on her multiplication tables was out of the question. I was feeling at a loss when Wally slinked into the room. At this hour, he liked to catch a snooze on the windowsill.

"A cat!" she exclaimed.

At last, something interesting at the meth house. But when she rushed toward Wally, he zigged and zagged and ran out of the room before she could even touch him.

"He's kind of shy. I don't think we'll catch him now. Come on, let's go somewhere."

She didn't have to be asked twice. The fields were too muddy for a hike, so we hopped in the Pontiac and started down the road. As we made our way to town, a ride of about ten minutes, she was silent until she said in a soft voice, "There's trouble at the mall."

I looked over at her but she stared straight ahead, watching the fence posts slip by.

"Oh, don't worry. I'm sure it'll get sorted out."

I flicked on the wipers, because it had begun to drizzle, and found myself thinking about Ginny's nickname, Bughouse. Or sometimes Amy called her Buggy. It was surely a reference to the song and dance but now it struck me as appropriate in other ways, too. She looked very small and inconsequential, sitting in my front seat. She was just a bug and anybody, *anybody* could squash her.

"Where we going?" she asked.

"It's a surprise," I said.

I didn't know myself, but the options in Legion were limited. As if on automatic pilot the Pontiac made its way to the school, and by the time we stopped in the parking lot and I turned off the engine, I had a plan.

"What are we doing here?" she asked.

"Have you ever been in school when everything's closed?"

She shook her head.

"It's *spooky.*"

She was unconvinced, but followed me to the loading dock in back, where I could use my passkey. We went through the utility area to a ground floor hallway, which was lit only by the stairwell windows at either end. *"Whooooo,"* I said, *"here pass the wandering souls of lost children,"* and she giggled. She began to play along, trying doorknobs as we roamed—the squeak of our shoes in the dimness produced a slightly eerie effect—and, eventually, we wound up in the gym. I didn't have access to the equipment room to get a basketball, but there was a recess supply bin in the corner and we took a bouncy kickball and improvised with that. It caromed wildly off the walls and basketball hoops, and soon we settled under one hoop with its pig-silhouette backboard and began to play, appropriately enough, a game of "pig." When Ginny attempted a shot that was far for her, she gave a frantic shuffle of her feet, and then launched the ball with a shoveling heave. She was on the verge of such a shot when, suddenly, she stopped and pointed. "There's a man!"

"Huh?" I turned around. I didn't see anyone. "No there isn't."

Ginny shook her head, clutching the ball in front of her. "There was! I swear I saw him!"

She seemed in earnest; this wasn't like our earlier game. Then the door squeaked and I whirled around.

It was Nelson.

"Hey there!" he said, approaching with both hands in his pockets. "I thought I heard voices. What's going on?"

There were brief introductions, and I could tell that Nelson was sizing us up, in light of my earlier conversation with him about Amy. I felt a little sheepish, and it took a minute before it occurred to me to ask, "What are you doing at school today?"

"Oh, just sorting out some supplies, getting set up for Monday morning. It's not so unusual to come in on a Saturday."

I knew that this was true, but even so he sounded defensive, and at this moment seemed less conscientious than very, very lonely. He stood looking at us with his hands in his pockets, and a silence stretched. On the overhead clock, the minute hand jerked forward, trembling. "Wanna play?" I asked.

He shrugged. "Oh, why not?"

And so for the next hour or so we kept at it, branching out to a game of "horse," and Nelson tried to teach Ginny how to spin a ball on her finger. Eventually we exited the school and parted ways with Nelson and went to Leroy's Supermarket, where we picked out a frozen raspberry dessert that we could have back at my place. Ginny was very quiet, almost sullen, and I could tell that she wanted to go straight home; but she had the guts not to come out and say so. Fortunately, Amy arrived not too much later at my place. She had a stern expression as she watched Ginny put on her coat.

"Thank you, Stanley. I'm sorry to have imposed. Where are your gloves?" she asked Ginny, who ran to fetch them.

"Is everything all right?" I asked.

"Absolutely. I'll tell you all about it later."

And then they were out the door.

❧

IT WAS time to open our science books to the health unit.

"Page 44, everybody! Is everybody there? Page 44. Hey, turn around! Stop it! Page 44. Hang on, not yet. Page 44. No. No. *No!* All right. Page 44. Listen up, everybody. Today we begin Dental Awareness Week."

Already this year I'd peppered my class with information about burns, beestings and heat exhaustion; I'd warned them about fish hooks, tick bites and drowning. In the future they could look forward to units on lead poisoning and food safety. Many of my kids still couldn't add and subtract properly, but they were successfully indoctrinated with a sense of life as something akin to running across a minefield.

"Mr. Mercer, look!"

Brain Rush gave me a thumbs-up. But not exactly—he was displaying his thumb, which was black. It appeared to have been dipped in ink. "What?" I said.

"I put this rubber band around it just before recess," he said, panting slightly, "a bunch of times, tight, and see what it does? The circulation has been cut off for like, I don't know, half an hour?"

I moved straight to his desk, and insisted that he remove the rubber band, because it was only a matter of time before he talked himself unconscious. We'd been down that road before. Woozily he took it off, and I went back to the front of the classroom and resumed the lesson.

For Dental Awareness Week, the state-supplied kit included a color poster about how to brush ("*Ignore Your Teeth, and They'll Go Away*"); a chart about the perils of gum disease (no photos, fortunately); a demonstrator toothbrush and a dreary educational game called "Match the Smiles," based on photographs of beaming celebrities with moveable strips at their lips. On all the materials, there was a conspicuous logo for a toothpaste brand which co-sponsored the Dental Awareness unit. At the end of the lesson, I passed out green cards.

"Now you take these home to your parents and make sure they get filled in," I advised, counting out the cards. On each was a preprinted schedule for regular dental checkups, along with a space for the dentist's signature. It was fairly certain that many of my kids rarely went to the dentist, or never did, because their parents didn't have insurance. "Everybody understand?" They all nodded. It was hard to say how much I'd enhanced Dental Awareness, but it was a pretty good lesson in hypocrisy.

Finally the bell rang and my pupils hurried out for lunch. "Don't run!" I yelled half-heartedly, watching them push and jostle. On my way out, I jumped up and grabbed a ceiling pipe, intending to do some pull-ups. This was a favorite spot, the same place where I'd grabbed 100 times before. It had become a habit, a way to unwind at work. But this time, on my first pull, the pipe suddenly broke off in my hands and I fell backwards onto the floor.

"Whoa!"

Rusty water gushed out, splashing on me and the wall. "Oh, shit!" I struggled to my feet and, fortunately, the flow of water dissipated, and soon became a trickle. Later, I learned that these pipes were part of an older system, no longer in use, but the first impression was alarming. Even after the water stopped, a huge puddle spread across the classroom floor while I reached up and tried to wedge the pipe back into place. But I couldn't make it stay. "Damn!"

I spent the lunch break mopping up and wiping down the pupils' desks in anticipation of their return. While cleaning the streaks of rusty water off the wall with a sponge, I took down the U.S. map and the picture postcards that had gotten splashed. They were stained and I decided to throw them away. I dropped the lot in the wastebasket and a short time later, rubbing with my sponge, I wiped away the last trace in this room of Nancy Heffernan.

❧

THE NEXT Saturday brought more damn rain and I didn't feel like going anywhere. I was sitting in my bathrobe at the kitchen table, scribbling on the back of a junk mail envelope, a few lines about how the bell at the monastery had sounded last summer when I woke up under a tree in Tauzé-le-Mignon and I'd risen, utterly at a loss, out of the dust. I couldn't say why I was writing this out, because it served no purpose, but that morning it suddenly seemed important to put it down in a way that left nothing to be desired, and the envelope was the closest paper at hand. I was looking at the words, lost to the world, when I heard a car door slam outside the house. This startled me.

Uh oh.

Funny, how the sound carried. *Amy, leave me alone!* I thought. I moved quickly to the window, and was relieved to see that it was someone else. A man was walking away from a mud-spattered, turquoise Ford. A moment later, the front door banged under a fist.

I retied my bathrobe. When I opened the door, a tall man stood scowling, holding a pair of sunglasses close to his mouth, chewing on a tip. Now I recognized him, from the real estate signs. It was Reggie Rawlings.

"Are you Stanley Mercer?" he asked.

"Yes."

We stared at each other for a moment.

"Is Amy here?" he said.

"No."

"So you admit that you know her," he pursued. "Would you care to tell me how?"

"Not really," I said.

My body tensed and my pulse began to pound. I'd heard nothing from Amy since she'd picked up Ginny last week. She'd said that she would explain later, but she hadn't contacted me. This was no surprise. And frankly, I didn't *want* to know. Good riddance. But now Reggie stood on my doorstep, looking upset. Shit, I thought. This day had to come.

"Do you know where she is?" he asked.

"Listen, Reggie, you'll have to sort that out for yourself. You'd better go."

"So you know who I am, too. I think we need to talk. That's not asking so much. Or are you afraid to let me in?"

"I'm not afraid of you," I said, opening the door.

Stupid of me, to accept his challenge. It was even more stupid when he stepped into my kitchen, and I found myself taking into account how shabby my house might appear to Reggie Rawlings.

"Decorated it myself," I said, with an ironic sweep of my hand. "A fix-me-upper. What do you think?"

Without being invited, he sat heavily on a kitchen chair, put his hands on his knees and stared at them. For a long moment he said nothing. He looked as if he might begin to cry. And I sure wasn't ready for that, either. It was a stretch to think of myself comforting *him*. "You want some coffee?" I asked. "Or a beer?" I moved toward the refrigerator, but stopped short. "Or are you allowed that? I got orange juice."

He looked up from his hands, unclenching his jaw. "Screw your orange juice."

"Huh?"

I'd heard him clearly but it seemed a ridiculous thing to say, and I was wondering where this could go next when he repeated himself, louder, and suddenly, clear as a shot, I understood. I'd been mistaken about many things, but the truth hit me straight on. "You're using again, aren't you? You're high."

"That's none of your fucking business," he said, with a put-upon righteousness that confirmed my words. His jaw worked back and forth and he seemed to be ticking things through in his mind. He scratched at his elbow. "If anybody else had done to me what I've done to myself, I'd shoot the son-of-a-bitch." Now he looked up again. "What do you and Amy do in Kingler-by-the-Sea? What the hell *is* Kingler-by-the-Sea? Those emails don't even make sense."

Ah, I thought. That's how you found out. I'd contacted Amy via her website a number of times.

"If you look at the dates on those emails," I said, "you'll see that we haven't been in touch for a while now. This is old stuff, Reggie. Let it go."

"What's happened to her inventory, dillweed?"

He picked up a salt shaker from the table, playing with the screw-top.

"I don't know what you're talking about."

"Nothing adds up at the store. Inventory is missing. The books at Tivoli's are worthless. She was padding her sales totals by buying her own stuff—*retail*. She paid with her own credit card. Jesus Christ! How smart is that? Was that your strategy?"

I pointed to the door. "That's the way out, Reggie."

He gave a disdainful shrug, got up from his chair and peered into the living room. "She had to stash that inventory somewhere. I could have the cops on your ass so fast your head would spin."

"Oh, for God's sake. There's nothing of Amy's here."

He turned back, now looking at the bottom of the staircase.

"I don't trust you. I'm gonna see for myself."

He started tromping up the stairs.

This really made me mad. If Reggie Rawlings didn't belong in my kitchen, he was even more out of place up there. But, short of grabbing him by the shirt or tackling him on the staircase, there was no good way to stop him. And I sure as hell wasn't going to follow and give him a tour. I folded my arms and waited. I heard floorboards creak, and the jangle of hangers as he checked my closet. For all I knew he looked under the bed, too. Goddamn it! This *was* too much. I went to the living room, where my unassembled curtain kit still lay in a corner, and I grabbed the thick wooden rod. Then I took a place at the bottom of the stairs. "Come down from there!"

"What the hell are all these boxes?"

Now he was in the bedroom where some of Nelson's possessions were stored. I heard a *thump*, then silence, and then another *thump*. He was moving boxes around, probably opening them as he went. I shouted at him again, and was on the verge of going up the steps and forcibly evicting him when he came pitching down the narrow stairwell. He drew up short when he saw me. I gripped the curtain rod like a bat.

"Get out of my house, dumbass," I said. "You caused Amy enough trouble already."

"This is fucked up!" he exclaimed, lifting his arms, tears rolling down his cheeks. "Those aren't clothes. What's all this shit? This is really fucked up."

"You're right about that," I said, and took a step toward him, and swung hard, aiming just above his head. Close enough for Reggie to feel the *whish* of parting air. He reeled back, and then ran for the door. I followed him out into the yard, where it had begun to rain again. The air smelled bad, too. He slipped on the wet grass but regained his footing and climbed into his Ford. Tires spinning, the car bounced out of my yard. I turned away, looking out over the fields, and then with a shout of disgust I threw the rod with all my strength across the yard and beyond the house, into the weeds of the orchard.

❦

ALL THAT evening, my nerves jangled, and I wondered if I should call Amy. Let her know what had happened. I straightened up the mess he'd made upstairs—Nelson had old gilt altar candlesticks, which were heavy, and vintage 1900s sheet music of lusty, comic songs from a time which no longer existed—and, in my bedroom, I discovered that Reggie had forgotten his sunglasses. He'd left them on the upstairs dresser.

In the end I decided not to contact Amy.

Let the Rawlings stew in their own juices, I thought.

❦

THE NEXT morning, I was drinking a cup of strong coffee in the kitchen and running my hand across my stubbly face, when my thoughts were interrupted by the sound of a fist pounding at my door. Two sharp blows, a pause, then two more.

For Christ's sake, *again?* I stood up so quickly that my chair almost fell over backwards behind me. And if Reggie had returned—oh, this could get ugly. Maybe he was going to try something. Maybe he wanted to raise the stakes. Yesterday I'd had no real intention of hurting the guy; I was merely trying to scare him away.

I edged across the kitchen, and peered at an angle out of the front windows. Instead of Reggie's turquoise Ford, there was a police car.

Oh, fuck, I thought. What's happened?

I hurried to the door.

"Mornin'," I said, blinking. "What can I do for you?"

"Wake you up?"

The police officer grinned, as if he'd said something amusing. He was a red-haired man of sturdy build. A light drizzle glistened on the shoulders of his jacket.

"No, I'm up. Is something the matter?"

"There's trouble at the Double Dee. The lagoons broke last night. It's all these rains lately. The spill ran down the creek bed and washed into the river, a couple hundred thousand gallons of sewage. I'm here to tell you to stay away from the river. You are now officially notified. You ever fish there?"

"Yeah. Not lately."

"Well, I don't think you'll go back there for a while. The state wants us to help out with some water samples to test for phosphorous and selenium. I'm supposed to bag some fish, too, so I'm gonna have to walk across this property."

"Makes no difference to me. I'm only a renter."

He grinned again. "I know that. Just being polite. I'm Alvin, by the way."

"I'm Stan Mercer."

"Yeah, I know that. You're the teacher. They used to run meth out of this house," he said.

"I know that."

He looked out beyond my yard, then turned back and asked, "Say, could you tell me the best access down there? It's awful muddy and I wouldn't mind saving these boots if I could."

I knew a good route through the orchard but it was hard to describe, and by now the drizzle had turned into a light rain.

"I'll show you," I said. "Give me a minute to get dressed."

He waited in the kitchen while I got ready. On the back steps I pulled on boots and zipped my coat and we walked squishing across the sodden lawn and through the taller grass of the orchard, where apple trees were in blossom. We climbed a fence and followed the slope toward the river.

"It's nice country around here," he said. "Real pretty. I'd like to get myself an acreage."

We avoided most of the mud till we came to a marshy area where it was impossible to put a foot on firm ground. The soil had a distinctive smell, not sweet, yet rich enough that you could imagine tasting it. Through a clearing in the trees I could see that the river had left its banks entirely, flooding a field. A flock of birds wheeled above the water, then came to rest in scattered knots on protruding limbs and weed stalks.

We climbed from the marsh to higher ground on the bank where foxtail grass swished at our knees. When I looked down into the river, the problem was obvious.

Dead fish bobbed in the current, their white bellies like huge flecks of spit. The water was cloudy and brown, some of it silt carried by the rains but in other places, it was thicker. A sludgy, dark, noxious cream.

"Whoa, look at that soup!" Alvin said. "Smell it?"

He pulled on a pair of latex gloves, and then tried to descend toward the water. He stepped gingerly because the ground was slippery and treacherous here. Part of the river-bank had crumbled into the river. For an instant the earth moved under him and I thought he might fall in. He called back over his shoulder.

"Gimme a hand, will you?"

So I grabbed a nearby willow branch, planted my feet firmly, and extended an arm, gripping the back of his jacket while he leaned over the water to scoop out a sample. For several seconds he was at my mercy: if I let go, it would've been like dropping a man into a giant unflushed toilet.

Not that I desired to watch. Craning my neck, I looked at clouds hurrying across the sky, as if fleeing the scene. I took short, gulping breaths, trying not to inhale too deeply.

"Okay! Got it!" Alvin shouted. "Pull me up!" With a jerk, we stumbled up to higher ground. "Goddamn!" he exclaimed. "What was I thinking? I shoulda brought a face mask."

He screwed the cap on the vial, and then gave it to me to hold while he went to collect some fish. This proved easy, because the current had crested during the night and a bend in the riverbank was littered with debris. A coffee-like coating clung to leaves and stalks and, in some bushes, dead fish hung like scaly fruit. Alvin took out a cellophane sandwich bag, turned it inside-out and plucked a fish. He wrapped it carefully and sealed the top. Then he repeated the action with several more. "There we go!" He took out a felt-tip marker and noted the date and time on the bag.

"Yeah," I said. "Clean country living."

Beginnings

9

The Cardiovascular Mobile, with its simulated blood circulation show and real human organs in formaldehyde, missed a corner on Highway 34 and ran into a tree. The driver telephoned Mr. Worthington from the police station in Brewton with the news that the Cardiovascular Mobile was out of commission.

So we were caught unprepared for Student Health Day. For lack of anything else to do, Mr. Worthington dismissed everyone from school for an hour to go outside and be healthy. This was a simple but effective solution, for it was not only warm but seasonably sweet, with a softness to the air. The playground was crowded and noisy with pupils burning off energy, while the teachers milled around on the edge of the grass, and a few chewed vigorously on nicotine gum.

Conversations buzzed with talk of last week's spill at the Double Dee, and in the first few days, I'd almost become accustomed to the *chunk-chunk-chunk* of helicopters passing over the pastures, as local TV stations sought out aerial views. Different versions of the accident circulated, as people tried to understand what had gone wrong. Was the spill the fault of the Double Dee, or was it the result of an unlucky chain of natural events, an unusually wet spring with late snows and heavy rains? The lagoon walls couldn't hold back the weight, and now some reports claimed that the spill was bigger than originally stated, with more than eight million gallons of liquid manure. There was also speculation about problems with the polyethylene liner surrounding the lagoon: seepage and gases from fermentation could've compromised the structure, long before the rains. But there was no certainty. Now that the accident had occurred, nobody in Legion had the right to go near the place, which was sealed off as a hazardous zone.

According to Mrs. Gordon, the Double Dee's manager had worked very hard to save the situation. In the days before the spill, he'd tried to offset the rains by pumping and spraying waste onto the nearby fields, as much as legal standards for fertilizer would allow. Later, when saturation had been reached, he'd stopped emptying the hog house pits. The problem, however, was that this measure couldn't be taken for too long, because the hogs kept shitting and shitting like clockwork, the pits filled up, until the waste rose up between the slats of the pens and the hogs were standing in their own excrement. The air inside the hog houses increased to over ninety degrees and became dense almost to the point of precipitation, and the manager feared for the safety of the animals and for the employees who entered the hog houses. He had no choice but to open the pipes that connected to the lagoon. Unfortunately, the expulsion pressure was so great that it created a wall-breaking surge. "He was working round the clock, doing everything humanly possible," said Mrs. Gordon. "You can't blame him."

"I hear they're trucking out the stock," said Rosemary Bird, a first grade teacher.

"That's right," said Mrs. Gordon. "And there goes the money, honey."

"Into everyone's life some rain must fall," mused Nelson. "Followed by a tidal wave of shit."

I ducked out of this conversation and moved away from the teachers, seeking a better way to spend the rest of the hour. My own pupils had scattered, generally segregating themselves into boys and girls, and from there into smaller groups, based on their affinities. I noticed that Ginny Rawlings was part of a little clique led by a bossy girl named Alex who presided, not too cruelly, as far as I could tell, over her disciples. I still hadn't heard anything from Amy since my encounter with

Reggie, and though I'd washed my hands of the parents, I still kept an interested eye on their daughter. Good thing Ginny had Colleen.

Shana had organized a game at the baseball diamond, so I walked toward her, cutting across the outfield. The right fielder was daydreaming, alone. He sucked on his glove and knelt in the grass, pulling off the heads of dandelions. Some low-flying swallows swooped and darted in the sunny air, occasionally pausing directly over him, making insane orbits above his head. When I passed he looked up, pulled out his glove, and wordlessly licked his lips. No one ever hit a ball out here. He was just someone's little brother whom they'd stuck out in right field. He probably thought he'd be a right fielder all his life. He decapitated another blossom, and stuck the stitched corner of the glove back into his mouth. I imagined the leathery tang.

Shana stood behind the backstop, watching the children through the wire mesh. "Well well," she said, "look who's here." We'd spoken several times about setting up a game with her kids, but we hadn't got round to it.

"Looks like you started without me," I said.

A swing, a crack of the bat, and the ball dribbled across the infield. After a couple of errors, the runner ended up on second base. The second baseman was a wiry girl named Doris. Shana had assembled a mixture of her students and other kids. Christine was a left fielder, with one hand lifted to shield her eyes from the sun, the other hand holding her glove over a breast. She looked bored.

I watched Jim Snow pick up a bat and walk toward the plate. A boy from the bus route was pitching, the kid with scraggly sideburns. T.J. was his name. I don't know what the initials stood for; everybody just called him T.J. People sometimes referred to an older brother of his who had famously suffocated by drowning in a bin of shelled corn. The dead brother was Bobby B.

T.J.'s first pitch was a slow, easy lob. Jim swung too early and missed it by three feet. T.J. grinned broadly, rubbed his glove on his thigh.

Jim looked back at Shana, and she nodded as if to say everything was all right. He turned back to the diamond. In spite of myself, I felt a strong desire to watch Jim take his swings. I'd tried to swear off this game. A person could scarcely conceive of a lower level. Still, I was drawn in. I couldn't help it. The next pitch was fast—a sucker set-up—Jim missed again.

This time T.J. laughed in his face. "I can feel your breeze from here, Jimbo boy!" He shook his arm at his side, limbering up for the next pitch.

"Idiot," Shana muttered. I wanted her to intervene, tell T.J. to slow it down and have some consideration for Jim. But she was silent. For the moment, she was not willing to single him out.

"Are you ready, Jimbo?" he asked.

Jim said nothing. The bat, an old taped wooden model that he'd chosen instead of an aluminum one, looked tiny and unintimidating in his hands. The color reminded me of a pencil.

T.J. wound up, kicked his leg, and delivered another fast one. It was high and wild, but Jim swung anyway, a desperate uppercut, and I was surprised by the sound of hickory, not a loud crack this time, but a more solid sound, shorter and deeper, like the blow of a wooden mallet on the head of a stake. *Tac!* Jim's body jerked; there was a hitch in his momentum before he followed through. Oh, I knew that sound! A beautiful sound. I leaned closer. The ball was sailing with tremendous velocity out to right field. The players turned to watch it fly.

Meanwhile, the right fielder still sucked on his baseball glove. The ball soared over his head, above the swallows, and he paid no notice. When, a moment later, he heard the cries of the infielders calling to him, he looked up, confused. They were pointing. He turned around in time to see the ball land and bounce. He threw down his glove and ran after the ball.

The center fielder joined in the chase. If I hadn't seen it myself, I would never have believed that Jim could hit a ball so far. Especially in these crude conditions. The ball rolled all the way to the swing sets, where Mr. Worthington walked alone with his hands in his pockets amongst the bare legs of little girls. It rolled across his path and he stepped back, startled.

And then I noticed that Jim still stood at the plate, watching the action. He could've circled the bases by now, but he hadn't moved a step.

"Run!" I called.

Shana grabbed my arm. Jim turned toward us, nodded, and tossed his bat aside. He jogged toward first base.

"He's okay," said Shana. "He knows."

She released her grip and we watched him. He clapped his hands as he loped around the infield. He let out a whoop. I'd never seen him so glad. There was something pure in his pleasure, and I felt it too—just watching him gave me hope. Even if it was only a game, a makeshift affair, for the moment at least, the world was upside-down, and it felt absolutely necessary.

The center fielder ran the ball in, getting close enough to make a throw. I wanted Jim to move faster, to avoid a close play. But on his way to third base he saw Christine in left field, and he waved, slowed down. Come on, I thought. Come on! The center fielder began the relay.

It was a good throw. The shortstop caught it, whirled, and fired the ball home.

But there was no play at the plate. The catcher caught the ball and looked out to left field, where Jim had strolled to talk to Christine. They began to walk away. The bell rang. Shana clicked her throat. I turned to her, and she seemed pleased.

☾

At the new mall, I looked for a wedding present for my mother and Archie. In Legion I'd failed to find anything appropriate. In the housewares department of a store called Olafson's, I deliberated over cutlery and rotisserie kits, and eventually opted for a set of crystal champagne glasses. That was at least in the spirit of things.

Then, with my package under my arm, I left Olafson's and followed the mall concourse toward Tivoli's. Although Amy had told me not to come to the store, that was back in the old days, when we were still secretly seeing each other. Now the circumstances were different. I would go wherever I damn well pleased.

But Tivoli's was closed. The metallic grate was pulled down. This wasn't, for me, a big surprise. I'd suspected that there was some substance to Reggie's ravings, the day he'd visited me. The store must've been badly managed. I went up to the darkened windows and peered inside. There were still racks of clothes—the place hadn't been cleared out. A voice called to me, "You want something?"

I turned, and saw a pretty young Asian woman at the earring kiosk. She sat on a high stool, watching me.

"Has this store been closed for long?" I asked.

"It was closed a lot when it was open. Maybe it still is. Who's to say?"

I approached her. "I thought you might say. You probably see when it's doing business."

She shrugged. "Lots of places are struggling. It's all the competition from the new mall."

This puzzled me. "Isn't this the new mall?"

She shook her head and explained in the tone that one would use for a simpleton that this *used to be* the new mall, but now there was a newer mall called Waveland Court, only two exits farther down the interstate. The malls at Valley West and Jordan Creek were feeling the pinch, too, and Merle Hay Mall was almost finished. Southridge Mall, she wasn't sure. There were rumors that this mall might be cut up into a number of mini-malls. Now she waved to a passing security guard with a squawking walkie-talkie on his belt, who waved back, leering at her. "What do you want?" she asked me. "You're not a customer, are you?"

"I wanted to speak to Amy Rawlings," and, when she made no reply, I added, "I'm a friend."

She shrugged. "Then call her. She's in the book."

As we parted company and I went on my way, my voice echoed in my head: *I'm a friend.*

At some basic level, was that still true? Did I mean it? Wasn't the knowledge that Reggie was getting high again a source of worry—worry about *her*? This occupied my thoughts while I went to a men's store and picked out a suit for my mother's wedding, and weighed on me in the car on the way back to Legion. After dinner, I decided to take action, and reached for the phone. The old taboo about calling Amy at home didn't mean much anymore, did it? She answered after two rings.

"It's Stanley," I said. "I just wanted to check in, make sure you're okay."

"Could be better."

Silence.

"Reggie's not giving you trouble, is he? What's the deal?"

"You tell me. I haven't seen much of him. My guess is that he's got himself a nice rock to smoke and he's holed up in a motel somewhere with it, having a good old time. He's with his true love now. There's no stopping him when he's like this. He's called a few times to talk, mainly to blame me for everything. God, he can be nasty."

"There's no reason to put up with that."

"Easy for you to say. He's contacted Sheila, too, and it really upsets her parents. He calls at weird hours because he doesn't sleep. When I heard the phone just now I thought it might be him. You know, he was clean till he found out about us. He was sticking to the program, calling his sponsor, the whole bit. But when he learned about us, he just said fuck it and went off the rails. He's going down fast."

"Every addict finds excuses. You know that. Look how he lied to you before! It's not your fault, Amy."

As we went back and forth and I tried to console her, sometimes I had trouble believing my own words. Yes, Reggie would have to face his problem—but wasn't it possible that he would still be on the right track, maintaining his recovery, if not for our actions? If he were on his way to ending up like his girlfriend Sheila, broken and invalid—or even dead—hadn't we, in our way, contributed? He might've done the same thing in other circumstances. On the other hand, he might've *not*. And now other circumstances weren't possible; he would never know them. We had done what we had done.

"You're right," Amy eventually said. "It's just bullshit when Reggie says I was never totally loyal to him. I've stood up for him. I'm not a quitter. It's not the way I'm wired. And I do think he'll understand that eventually, and come back with his tail between his legs."

"Well—and what then?"

"It's not like he has many choices! He has to get his shit together. His parents have found a residential treatment center in Kansas City that can take him now, there's a place for him. The trick is to get him to want to go. You wouldn't believe what I've been going through lately. I'm just stuck to the phone, afraid of what I'm going to hear next. I hardly leave the house."

I mentioned that I'd been to the mall on an errand, and had noticed that Tivoli's was closed.

"Oh, that, too. Business has been poor. That's beyond my control."

"I'm sure the new mall hasn't helped your situation any, either."

"Exactly. Listen, Stanley. I need to ask you a question. You have to be straight with me."

"Sure. What?"

"Is it true that you went after Reggie with a baseball bat?"

This caught me by surprise. "Huh?"

"He says all kinds of things and I don't know what to believe anymore. I'm going to trust you to tell me the truth about what happened."

"Well, actually, it was a curtain rod. He'd come looking for you. He also said he was looking for missing inventory from your store."

The line went silent. Eventually I added, "Amy, he was being a big-time jerk. He was tramping all over my place!"

"That was really stupid, Stanley."

"You didn't see it. He was totally flying!"

"What were you thinking? Do you see how that weakens my position? Reggie's not the victim here."

"I couldn't agree more."

"But he'll use this against me, I know he will. And don't believe anything he tells you about the store. There are two sides to that story. Oh, I can see what's coming. He'll get his parents to put their lawyers on me if I go through with a divorce. They'll make sure that I get stuck with almost nothing. They've never respected me. They've got a silver spoon up their ass."

This made me angry, though I couldn't find the right words to say why. Was *that* her worry? "To hell with Reggie's parents. And to hell with Tivoli's. None of those are the problem."

"Not *your* problem. Why are you calling, Stanley? What do you want from me? This entire conversation makes me feel weird, you know that? What it's about? It's like you're making a claim for something that's already over, for something you never had. You have no claim to make. Not with *me*. Understand?"

"I understand," I said, "but there are other considerations, for God's sake. What about Ginny?"

This really set her off. She exploded: "What about her? What do you know? You have any kids? Fuck you, Stanley! Fuck you in both ears! Fuck your stupid little life. Your stupid little face, Jesus—right now—I could—*smash* it. God! How *dare* you bring Ginny into this. Like you care? Or know something? All those Sunday afternoons when I was with you, where do you think Reggie supposed I was? He thought I was with Ginny. You ever wonder about that? Or were you just too distracted by that hard-on in your pants? You're the last person who should lecture me. Oh, Lord. What hypocrisy!"

And then, abruptly, our conversation ended. I can't say who hung up first. It was as if, on this matter at least, we'd reached a consensus. We hung up at the same time.

❧

It was warm enough now to leave the windows open at night and to hear insects batting against the wire screens. I lay in darkness in the company of images projected at the back of my weary skull, as in some haunted drive-in theater in the middle of an abandoned field that kept running and running and refused to shut down. I listened to the night sounds and wished it would stop.

Once, at Kingler-by-the-Sea, Amy and I had spent an afternoon together, both in the room and by the pool, after which we showered and dressed, getting ready to leave again. Amy had just finished using the hair dryer and now she sat on the edge of the bed with one shoe on, one shoe off. "Gosh, my eyes are tired," she said, blinking. "Maybe it's the chlorine. I really don't want to face that drive." She dropped the shoe in her hand, kicked off the shoe on her foot, and fell back on the bed. "Let's just rest for a couple of minutes. Five minutes, let me close my eyes."

She curled on her side and, a moment later, I joined her, both of us fully clothed and lying on top of the bedspread. I nestled behind, pulled her against my chest. I listened to her breathe and tried to keep still, and not disturb her. There was nothing particularly sexual; this little nap seemed of a different order. I felt a sudden stab of tenderness for her. For the first time, I felt like making an avowal. I wanted to express this tenderness. To say *I love you* would've surprised her, and probably perceived as excessive. (Or, I wondered at the time, was it merely premature?) But the tenderness was there, it was real. How I should tell her, I wasn't sure: but I knew what I longed to hear. The same tenderness in return.

She'd fallen fast asleep.

I listened to the hum of the heater and then I must've dozed myself. It was a delicious nap; time escaped us entirely—or, rather, we escaped time. How long we slept was hard to say but when I awoke, the room was noticeably dimmer. Again, the hum of the heater. I didn't move, trying, by doing nothing, to return to the previous state. After a while I became aware that she was awake, too. But she wasn't moving.

Eventually she rose to her knees and looked down on me. "It's so late, Stanley, I really have to go. Stay and sleep if you want to." She ran her hand through my hair. "Be good." And there was tenderness in the gesture.

Then she jumped down from the bed, found her shoes and coat, and was out the door.

Now, at the meth house, the first stirrings of birds came before dawn, audible on the other side of the screen, and it was obvious that any tenderness we'd shared was irretrievable and that, given the way we'd carried on, was more than we deserved. *Be good*, indeed. A new day was waiting, for us and for this place, and what would be more necessary in this bughouse world?

10

At the Bernie Barbecue Mr. Worthington sported a new moustache, and he wore shorts, revealing smooth, girlish legs. He stood at the grill with a pair of tongs, keeping an eye on the pork chops, while Mrs. Worthington waited nearby with a platter of bratwurst. She was a surprisingly young, attractive woman with a pale squinting face, like someone who'd misplaced her glasses.

Teachers and spouses milled in little groups, and many people had brought their children. A pair of toddlers sat on their blanket as upright as penguins, and fluttered their arms at their sides. A frisbee soared and landed in a flower bed. A man named Rodney was doing sit-ups on the grass, I had no idea why. Nelson was at the end of the yard, playing lawn darts (he waved impatiently at me to come and join him, but I turned away) while Chadwick, gripping a can of soda in each hand, stood next to his wife, a smiling, round woman with a wooden cross on a leather thong around her neck. They were speaking to Les McGee, the janitor. This gathering was an annual show of unity, which was beginning to feel as mythical as Bernie himself, since today much of the conversation centered, as it often did lately, on the spill at the Double Dee, which had become a prickly subject.

"Now's the time we all have to pull together," Mrs. Gordon said. "This situation doesn't have to be a total loss. The important thing is to address the damage and set things safe so that they'll bring back the stock and get operations going again. The layoffs can be temporary."

"Get things going, and risk another spill?" Shana said. "It's not just the river. What if the aquifer is contaminated, too? When does it stop?"

I'd paused with my plate in front of a table of covered dishes, intending to load up, and I'd walked straight into an argument.

"You hear that, Stanley?" said Mrs. Gordon. "That's simply alarmist. That's the kind of foolish thing they put out in the media and people start repeating it, in total disregard of the facts. To date there is no proof of that happening here. Zero proof. Did you know that?"

I shook my head, and began to scoop faster.

"Well, I'm just saying—" Shana began.

"What's your source?"

"It's mentioned in the news, so I'm just saying."

"Get a scientific source."

"It's happened elsewhere, hasn't it?" I put in, looking up.

"But we're talking about here, aren't we? Or are you saying that we have a problem here but it's okay if we push it some-where else, make somebody else deal with it. 'Not in my back-yard,' is that what you're saying? Is that fair? Because that's what'll happen. Mark my words, the company will set up in another town, or another state. And Legion will be worse off for it. Anybody can play the blame game, but what next?"

"Listen, I know your husband works there," Shana said. "It's nothing personal. But I'm talking about the long run. Do we really want to have operations like the Double Dee anywhere?"

I licked some salsa off my fingers, and now Chadwick stepped up, bobbing his head in greeting. His wife was taking a call on her cell phone and he gravitated toward us the way a kid is drawn to a confrontation in the school yard.

"You're absolutely right, Shana, it's not about my hus-band," Mrs. Gordon retorted. "It's about what's good for the community. For our children."

"Yes, that's what I'm saying," Shana said. (Though it couldn't have been more clear that they disagreed.) "I simply don't approve of that kind of operation. I can't remember the last time I ate pork."

Mrs. Gordon laughed, slapping the side of her arm. "Oh dear, I should've known! Well, that's your right, honey. Suit yourself. But don't think you can dictate to everybody else what to do. We don't all have the same lifestyle. A bit of tolerance, please."

Shana's face went stony.

In a conciliatory tone, Chadwick said, "In ancient Egypt, the water turned to blood, and people had unhealable boils. There was a plague of locusts, and hail mixed with fire. Just think what Moses and the Israelites went through. We surely ought to be able to get through this."

Everyone blinked, and for a moment politely paused and pretended to ponder ancient Egypt. Chadwick looked around. He was aware that we didn't all share his ideas, but he pressed on: "I'm just saying, there's a big picture and everybody's a part of it. This is no time for the faint of heart. Our youth group at the New Tabernacle has adopted a section of the river to clean up the fish kill—you know the way they adopted part of the highway west of town to pick up trash? It's part of their witness to the community. The worst of it has already washed away and it's safe to go in."

"Washed where?" Shana said. "That's my question."

"Everybody understands that," Mrs. Gordon said. "We get it, okay? The point is, some of us are trying to be constructive. What we need now are people willing to roll up their sleeves."

"Hey, Mercer! Care to join me for a game?"

It was Nelson, calling across the green. He held a bunch of lawn darts in his fist like a bouquet.

I shook my head, but he persisted. "Come on, Stanley. Be manly!"

I used his interruption as a diversion to escape the others, but instead of going to Nelson, I headed for the grill. People stood in line, drumming their fingers on paper plates like tambourines, waiting to be served by Mr. Worthington. In the corner of my eye I saw Nelson striding toward me in pursuit. Would he never give up?

"Watch out for those tree huggers," he said as he drew near, "you'll get splinters in your dick. Stanley, we need to talk."

"What is it?"

He lifted his chin, made a flicking motion with his head. "I mean in private."

"Let me get some food first."

He stayed beside me as the line moved forward, as if I might try to slip away. "What's this all about?" I asked. He said nothing, but hung close, and then Mr. Worthington dropped a chop on my plate with a smile, saying, "It's boneless."

So I followed Nelson away from the people to a quiet corner of the yard that was decorated by a miniature Dutch windmill.

"All right—what?" I was fairly certain that I didn't want to hear it.

"Need to give you a head's up about your girlfriend. Do you know about her husband?"

I chewed and then swallowed. "Huh? If you mean the Rawlings woman, she's not my girlfriend. And her husband isn't my problem. I know he's a tweaker, if that's what you mean."

"Don't get all pissy on me, Stanley, I'm just the messenger here. You still might want to know something that happened this morning. This guy, Crenshaw, he goes mushrooming in Missouri every Spring and he always brings me back some, okay, and today I went to his place to pick them up? Well, when I get there, everybody's all upset because of a big scene next door. They're neighbors with the Rawlings kid and her grandma, and there'd been trouble. Seems the father showed up at the grandma's this morning and told her that he was taking the kid with him. Grandma must've told him to get lost. Anyhow there was an argument and Ginny comes running and crying through the Crenshaws' back door when they're still sitting around eating their cereal. They're wondering, what the hell? They know her because she plays with their kids. And while they're trying to calm her down and figure out what happened, the father shows up at the back door. He just walks right in. What's his name?"

"Reggie," I said.

"Reggie walks right in and tells Ginny to come with him and it's obvious she doesn't want to go. Phil Crenshaw said he seemed totally calm and normal, except that he's holding a telephone in his hand. Not a cell phone, but a telephone receiver with a cord hanging off it. Ripped off the wall. This was fucking weird and Marcia Crenshaw got the kids out of there, because their kids were watching this, too, and she told him Ginny would be waiting in the next room while they sorted it out. And she hustled them through the house and out the front door and they locked themselves in their car and just sat there in the driveway, while she called 911 on her cell. Meanwhile Phil is still with Reggie in the kitchen, and he said Reggie was explaining in all kinds of detail why it was time for Ginny to come home with him but Phil could hardly listen to a thing he was saying because he noticed a bunch of white hair sticking to the phone. Freaked him out. Marcia hadn't had time to see that. He didn't want to stare at it, the thing to do was to let Reggie keep talking, because he knew that Marcia would call the cops. It was only a matter of time. But he said it seemed like a mighty long conversation."

"Oh fuck. Just tell me what happened."

"She's still alive. They found her unconscious on the kitchen floor. Apparently, even after the cops arrived, Reggie didn't get excited or resist, he kept telling them that he'd come for his daughter, and that was all. It was like he expected the police to take his side, and hand Ginny over to him. Anyway, they arrested him, and they took Ginny in another car. They wouldn't let her stay with the Crenshaws since the Crenshaws aren't family. When I saw them this morning, all this had just happened and they were still chewing it over. They were in a state." Nelson paused, and looked past me toward the eating teachers. "Sorry, Stanley. But I thought you might want to know."

☾

W<small>HEN</small> I arrived at Eicher Memorial Hospital, there was no one at the reception desk, though staff workers in white hurried by in one direction or another, shoes squeaking on the linoleum. The place had the nervous energy of a basketball court. I knew Colleen's room number because I'd called in advance and tried to speak to her, and had been told they would connect me to room 211; but then another voice came on the line and informed me that it wasn't possible to talk to Mrs. Harrison, because her jaw was broken and had been wired shut.

So, after standing a couple of minutes at the reception desk without managing to speak to anyone, I ventured down the corridors in search of room 211. It wasn't hard to find.

Upon entering, I was relieved to see that Colleen had no other visitors. I felt no desire to bump into Amy or to make small talk with a stranger. Even so, we weren't alone. Colleen sat upright in bed with her back to a pillow, with part of her cranium shaved and bandaged, and her lips stretched tight into a forced smile. Next to the window in another bed a few yards away, an aged woman lay on her back, her mouth opening and closing, taking in air with audible gulps. It was fish-like. Ghastly. As I hesitated on the threshold, looking on, a nurse tapped me on the shoulder and obliged me to step into the room because she wanted to enter, too. First she trotted to Colleen's roommate, quickly looked her over, checking the chart at the foot of her bed and, seeming to find that all was well, she came to Colleen and inspected her bandage. During this time Colleen's eyes darted around, looking at me and then away again. The nurse asked, "You here to see Mrs. Harrison?"

"That's right."

"She can't say much. She can't say anything. You her son?"

"No. I'm a friend."

"Well, don't stay too long, it tires her."

Then she was out the door.

"Hello. You probably remember me. I'm Mr. Mercer, Ginny's teacher? I was really sorry to hear what happened. This is just—awful." Her eyes fixed on me again as I groped for words. It was one thing to come and pay my respects, but it was another thing to make a speech; I should have thought this through, and figured out more to say. I noticed the cut flowers in a vase next to her bed, no doubt the gift of an earlier visitor, perhaps Amy, and I considered saying that they were pretty, but decided that the remark would sound too feeble; so, for several seconds, we simply looked at each other.

A trolley rattled by in the corridor; the fluorescent light hummed overhead; and there was another faint sound, *pup . . . pup . . . pup,* which seemed to come from far away, some kind of engine or a construction noise from beyond the building; and I experienced a pang of longing for the world outside the hospital, these ammoniac walls, knowing that I'd be pleased to get the hell out of here, when my visit was done, and closer to that distant sound—until I realized that the sound was Colleen's roommate lying in the adjacent bed, opening and closing her mouth for air.

Now I rushed to speak: "So, anyway, I just wanted to stop by and see how you're doing. This has been a bad time, I know, but I hope things will get back on the right track. If there's anything I can do, I'd be glad to help. I'll leave you my number. You should know that everybody really appreciates what you've done for Ginny. She's been a real pleasure to have in class."

While I spoke she reached over to the nightstand and pulled a pad of paper onto her lap. Then she groped next to the vase of flowers. I came closer. "Here, let me get that for you." I handed her a ballpoint pen, clicking it down for her.

Colleen wrote quickly, with a sucking sound of saliva in her mouth. She held out the pad to me. Her handwriting was slanted but clear: *"I know about you. You're not my friend. Get out of here."*

☾

Mr. Worthington stuck his head in my classroom and asked, "Could you stop by my office when you've finished today?"

He startled me. Fortunately I was on the verge of passing out a test, so all my pupils were silent, heads up, in anticipation. The illusion was perfect. The moment he peered in, we looked as industrious as ants. No child left behind here, boss.

"Sure, no problem," I said.

His shining head withdrew, and I began to pass out the papers, walking between the rows of desks. I assumed that he wanted to see me about Ginny Rawlings, who was absent for the third straight day. (It wasn't a nice thought, but it would be good for the class average that her score wouldn't be included in our statistics.) My pupils began to scratch at their papers while I stood at the front of the room with my arms folded, watching them work. Inexorably my gaze was drawn up to the broken pipe in the ceiling. It gaped above the room like an exposed nerve. The atmosphere of this place was changed now. Funny how you could feel it. I became aware of pupils, too, as they twitched and chewed on their pencils, glancing up at the pipe: their faces strained, as if mentally trying to supply a connection.

Later, in Mr. Worthington's office, I asked, "What did you want to see me about?"

"Have a seat, Stanley."

He got up and closed the door, and then came back and sat down across from me.

"The superintendent is sending out the contracts for next year," he said. "There should be one for you, but first I have a question."

He paused, and I waited. Usually Mr. Worthington preferred to communicate by email. Even so, I wasn't particularly stressed or concerned. With hindsight, I realize that it was stupid of me to have been so unprepared for what came next.

"Do you, or do you not, have a bachelor's degree?"

There was a lawyerly precision to his question that required a precise answer. Plus, looking a person in the eye is not the same as filling out a form. I didn't even hesitate. I told the truth.

"No, I don't have one."

At these words, Mr. Worthington visibly wilted. For a moment I had the impression that I'd misunderstood his purpose, and that he would've preferred that I lie.

"The superintendent asked me to review your credentials. That's part of my job. You know that even a temporary teacher's certificate isn't possible without a bachelor's degree. Everyone knows that. This is bad, Stanley. We've got a problem. And not just for next year."

He sighed.

"What do you mean?"

"Okay. I relay this information to the superintendent. The superintendent has to terminate you. He can't do otherwise. We're not far from the end of the school year, though, so maybe you can finish. Maybe not. It won't be up to me. Getting a substitute for this last month is a lot of trouble. So I can't say what will happen. There's always an element of improvisation when the poop hits the fan."

I sat in silence, my thoughts scattered by the unexpected-ness of it all, and by the fact that he'd said "poop." It was hard to focus. Eventually I managed to ask, "Are you sure that this isn't about anything else?"

He was puzzled. "I think this ought to be enough, Stanley." Mr. Worthington mused for a moment. "It's possible that the superintendent could take it to the school board, to see if we should sue you."

"Sue me?"

"To pay us back for what you earned under false pre-tenses."

This last possibility was even more of a surprise. I must've blanched, because he lifted a hand, as if to stop my thoughts.

"This would be a kindness on his part, you understand, to play out the clock. They won't sue you because legal counsel costs too much money. But the superintendent will have raised the responsible question and, in the meantime, the school year finishes and we don't have to recruit a substitute. It's less messy, all around."

"I see. I think I see."

"It's not up to me, though. That's just one scenario. We'll have to wait and see what he does." Mr. Worthington looked at his watch. "I won't relay this information to him until tomorrow. That'll gain a day right there."

He paused, and perhaps I was supposed to thank him. But the words didn't come to me. The entire conversation was humiliating, as if I were some kid called on the carpet in the principal's office.

As I stood up to leave, he asked, "Why did you do it?"

"Because I wanted a job. You know, I almost have a degree. I was just a few credits short."

This last remark sounded needy, as if I were asking to be indulged, and as soon as I said it, I regretted it. He linked his fingers together. "All things considered," he said, "you haven't had a bad first year." He looked off into space, as if searching for something positive to say. It took him awhile, and eventually he told me, "The parents seem to like you."

〇

"THIS IS actually a good break," Beverly wrote in an email. "A shake-up can be salutary." ("Salutary" was one of her favorite words: her Tai chi class, she told me, was salutary. The effects of longer daylight hours and the change in seasons were salutary.) Over the winter we'd exchanged an occasional email, nothing very personal, but in recent weeks our correspondence had picked up. I didn't share a word about Amy or what had happened to Colleen; I wouldn't have known where to begin. Nor did I explain the reason why my job was coming to an end. I tried to sound jaunty about the situation. It was "my latest surprise," I wrote her, "an enforced vacation."

"What next?" she wrote back.

"Looks like the show will go on the road."

At school, I didn't mention this development to other teachers. It was embarrassing and I figured that they'd find out soon enough. The subject of next year's contracts had come up in conversation at the cafeteria, with people making sour jokes about salaries, but I didn't join in.

Late at night I got a phone call.

"Stanley, it's me. I have to talk to you. There are three things I have to tell you. All right? Are you listening?"

I sat up in bed, blinking. After our last conversation, when Amy had told me to fuck off in so many different ways, I'd assumed that we wouldn't be speaking again. "Yeah. I'm here."

"Okay. First, don't go near my mom. You're creeping me out. What are you, some kind of stalker?"

"Now wait a minute! It's not about you. I was just checking in with her. I felt bad about what happened."

"It's not your concern. Stay away from her. *Second*—are you listening?"

"What? Are you reading from a list?"

"Second, Ginny's back with me now, and she's going to have to enroll in a school up here. Colleen's not in any shape to take care of her."

"Of course not. How is Ginny?"

"I don't want to go into it with you, Stanley. She was pretty shaken up, as you can imagine. What she needs now is positive structure and a good school will help her with that. I've got a lead on a place that looks promising but she needs a letter of recommendation. That's the second thing I have to tell you."

By now my breaths were coming faster, but I managed to keep my tone even. "All right. You have told me. Mr. Mercer will consider it."

This answer seemed to unsettle Amy, for her tone changed as she continued: "I know her grades aren't as good as they should have been. I'm not asking you to say she's a genius or something. But you appreciate her, I can tell. This is not about us, Stanley. Think whatever you want of me, but surely you agree that Ginny should be in school, in the best school possible. This is Trilling Academy and it would be such an opportunity for her. I'm not knocking the job you've done in Legion. I'm sure you've tried your best. But if she had a more effective educational environment—"

"Don't push it, okay? I'll write Ginny a letter. For her sake. But don't make me listen to a pitch."

She was annoyed, I could tell, but she moved on. "Third, you're going to be approached and I should warn you about it. Reggie's in the county jail, which is right where he belongs, but his parents are working on getting him out on bail and into treatment again before he goes on trial. Now I know a thing or two about Reggie's parents. They're going to make this into something more than him answering to charges. They want to lay some groundwork for the divorce. Let me give you some friendly advice."

"Oh, Jesus," I said. "You're my friend now, are you?"

"Just hear me out," she said.

According to Amy, Reggie's parents wanted information about my relationship with her, because it could affect a judge's ruling in any future settlement. She said that Reggie's parents would exaggerate and twist things and she feared that she would get a bad deal for her and Ginny.

"Hey, I'm not going to talk to anyone about my personal life."

"Good—"

"But it's not because I give a damn about your divorce settlement. Listen, I have to go to work in the morning." And I put down the phone.

☾

A<small>MY WAS</small> right. The next morning I got a call from a Mr. Sullivan, who identified himself as an attorney representing Lawrence Rawlings. I told him I was busy, which was true. He said that he could come down and see me, at my convenience. I told him that if Mr. Rawlings had something to say to me, he could tell me personally, and not through a lawyer. Then I hung up on him.

Although I didn't trust Amy to give a reliable version of events, I was a little unnerved by this call. And that was only the beginning. Mr. Sullivan called again in the evening, and announced that both Mr. and Mrs. Rawlings could be available to meet me that weekend. I replied that I had plans to be out of town, which was true.

The next day, I'd been home from school for barely ten minutes and was making a snack in the kitchen when the sound of a car engine came through the screen windows; I moved toward the living room to look out, and a car door slammed. Wally whizzed across the back of the couch and ran behind the stereo. Another door slammed, and I saw two men walking across the yard, and a woman getting out of the car.

And here they were! Shit. This place was becoming a goddamn Rawlings' family reunion! I felt more than a little riled and immediately stepped outside, holding a sandwich in my hand, before they had a chance to knock. I didn't invite them in the house. Our conversation lasted about five minutes.

Mr. Rawlings was a tallish man in blue knit slacks and a polo shirt; he looked like a white-haired Reggie, with watery blue eyes, and just a little softer around the middle. The other man, who wore a dark suit and red tie, started by saying, "I'm Jim Sullivan—we spoke on the phone? This is Lawrence." He waited for Mr. Rawlings to shake my hand first. It would've been mildly hysterical on my part to refuse to shake hands, once they initiated the gesture, so I went along with it, while still holding a sandwich in my other hand. "And this is Dorothy," he continued, as a petite, plump woman in an ochre pantsuit came up from behind. She was still quite pretty, with auburn hair and, after we touched fingers, she kept a step back from the man. "We were in the area," Jim Sullivan said, "and thought we'd stop by, have a word with you."

"Just happened to be passing through, were you?" I asked.

"This kind of thing is unpleasant but it has to be addressed," said Mr. Rawlings. "If it could be avoided, I wouldn't bother you."

"Sometimes a simple conversation is all it takes," said Jim Sullivan.

I was uneasy, because this conversation seemed anything but simple. The Rawlings had brought along their lawyer and that smelled bad to me. What was I supposed to do, run out and get my own lawyer to argue my side? But what was my side? These people had already figured out their agenda. The smartest thing, I resolved, was to say as little as possible.

Sullivan did most of the talking. The issue at hand, he said, was the future custody of Ginny Rawlings. They had no intention of denying the mother her rights—that was not their purpose—but they believed that these rights were not exclusive, and that Reggie, who would have to answer for his actions in a court of law, had not, on the other hand, forfeited his rights forever, and that other parties, such as Lawrence and Dorothy, should not be excluded because of their son's errors—in fact, they could play a very constructive role in Ginny's life. "We understand that you know Amy Rawlings well," Sullivan pursued.

"Yes. I'm her daughter's teacher."

He nodded. "We also understand that you have met Amy Rawlings at her place of business, and in more personal situations."

"What is it that you want from me?" I asked.

His reply made it sound very simple, easy, and almost discreet. All they requested, he explained, was a deposition from me, acknowledging that I had been intimately involved with Amy Rawlings. There would be no need for explicit or uncomfortable details; mainly they wanted dates. And the purpose of this deposition was to clarify relevant circumstances for the welfare of Ginny Rawlings, with the goal of allowing other parties a place in an eventual custody arrangement.

"The mother should have a share of custody," Mr. Rawlings said. "We won't fight that. But it has to be fair. There's nothing personal against you, Mr. Mercer. But things have come to a pass. She's threatened to never let us see Ginny again. That's how she bargains. She's using the child for her own ends."

"I got a question," I said.

They shifted on their feet, and James Sullivan said, "Yes?"

"What about Colleen Harrison?"

Sullivan was the first to reply, saying that her situation was a matter of grave concern to everyone, and what had happened would always be a source of great regret, and it

was their heartfelt wish that a speedy recovery would be followed by a chance to renew their relationship, since they had
always held Colleen in high esteem. "With all due respect to
Mrs. Harrison and her suffering, Lawrence and Dorothy are
not responsible for what happened. And Reggie knows he's
going to have to answer for what he did."

"It's terrible. It's terrible," interrupted Mrs. Rawlings in
a choked voice. This was the first time she'd spoken, and
now tears were flowing down her cheeks. "Why would he
do that to Colleen? I still don't believe it. He's never tried to
hurt someone before. He's not really like that. This is like the
worst dream and it doesn't stop. Oh, Jesus." James Sullivan
fell silent for a moment, looking at the grass, and Mr. Rawlings went over and put an arm on his wife's shoulder. "Why
did all this happen?" she said. "They used to be such a nice
couple."

"I really doubt that," I said.

But this was merely a spiteful remark, irrelevant. Now
Dorothy Rawlings was sobbing, shaking, as if something had
broken loose inside her. Fresh tears leaked all the way down
to the corners of her mouth, where they stopped and accumu-
lated like the residue of her words. We stood awkwardly and
then, suddenly, she shook off her husband's arm and stepped
toward me, her entire body trembling, and said, "You can't
know my grief. Mister, you can't even begin to imagine." Then
she turned and stalked to the car, got in the backseat, and
slammed the door.

It's difficult to recall what happened next, because of
this distraction. Sullivan and Mr. Rawlings spoke some more
about the deposition, while Mrs. Rawlings waited in the backseat. The car windows were rolled up, so I couldn't hear her
sobs, but from where I stood, I could see her rocking back
and forth. Like a passenger on a bumpy ride, though the car
wasn't moving. How can he leave her in there like that? I
wondered. It was hard to concentrate on their words, or to

think of anything else. At this moment she was in hell. True, they were facing a different direction and couldn't see what I was seeing. And *I* was the one who'd stirred my finger in her wound. Despite my resolve, I'd said too much. Eventually I couldn't stand to watch or listen anymore, so I threw up my arms and told them, *"Can't do it."* I turned and went back in the house.

11

 $\mathbb{M}$ y mother's wedding was at three-thirty on Saturday afternoon. After work on Friday I went home briefly to put out some food for Wally, and then hurried to load up my Pontiac for Chicago. I put the champagne glasses in the trunk, where I also lay out my suit bag and a gift-wrapped package for my new niece, Ruthie, who was barely ten days old. I'd been uncertain of what kind of present would please Riley and Serena, who surely had everything they needed; finally I settled on a Bernie Bib, a bit of local paraphernalia sold by the Legion Sports Boosters. A kid always needed something to spit up on.

Soon I was speeding down the highway toward Beverly's.

Yes, Beverly's. When I'd mentioned in an email that I was coming to Chicago for a wedding, she invited me for a sleep-over. That was Beverly's exact term: a "sleepover." Oh, my my. After a brief hesitation, I accepted. "Sounds salutary," I wrote back.

And why not? Recent weeks had been a bad roller-coaster ride. It would be hard to sort out exactly how I felt about many events but one feeling I was sure of: fatigue. I wanted to rest my stupid brain. Short of solutions, I would settle for a respite.

She greeted me at her door with a big smile, and we hugged briefly.

"Good to see you, Stanley."

"How you doing, Binky?"

"Great." She stepped back into the vestibule to let me in, and the door thumped shut behind me. "You look tired, Stanley."

"It's been a busy time. You look good. Just the same."

"No I don't. I cut my hair."

"Except for that, of course," I said.

She laughed. "Oh, stop it." And, to my surprise, she stepped forward and hugged me again, this time firmly. It was nice, though I wondered: Geez, do I look *that* bad? But I squeezed her back. The feel of Beverly in my arms, those breasts against my chest, all that companionable femininity, was a relief and a tonic to me. I had no illusions, but this feeling was powerful. Beverly ran her hands on my shoulders, then around my waist. Maybe she was experiencing something similar. Even if I wasn't The Man, it could be good to be around a man. Maybe she needed that. Now she pulled down her purse from a shelf and fumbled inside and I wondered: *What's your story this past year, nice lady? Any wrecked lives?*

But there was nothing morose about Beverly tonight. She seemed in a jolly mood. She held up a key, smiling. "Come with me, Stan," she said, snapping her purse shut. "I want to show you something." She pushed past me out the front door and skipped down the steps. She pointed the key at a shiny car parked at the curb. The car chirped, and its lights flashed on. "What do you think?" she called. "Come on, get in."

I joined her, sliding into a leather seat. "Where are we going?" I asked.

"Nowhere. I just want you to see it. Smell that."

I took a breath.

"New car," I said.

"Isn't it fabulous? It's an Omega 600!"

"Wow," I said. In truth I knew nothing about this model but it was obviously very plush. "Snazzy."

"I won it!"

"No. Really?"

"My salary wouldn't pay for this, bub." She tilted the steering wheel down to her lap, adjusted the rear-view mirror, then ran her hand along the top of the dashboard. She literally petted it. "Isn't this amazing? See, I bought a DVD player after Christmas at Whitestone's and filled out a little card, sent it in? There was a drawing with lots of prizes. I always enter a contest when I see one. In the supermarket I fill out the cards when I wait in line, just to pass the time. And look what happened! Phone rings this morning, out of the blue—and bingo! They delivered it this afternoon and took a ton of pictures. Can you believe it?"

"It's great."

"This is the first time I ever won anything, except once in high school, a frozen turkey, and that was because I cheated." She leaned toward me, batted her eyes, and whispered, "My boyfriend Charlie worked at the store." Then she leaned back and drummed her hands happily on the steering wheel. She honked the horn. "*Whoooo!* Isn't it amazing?"

Such high spirits were contagious, and I leaned over and kissed her. She pulled away, laughing, then she leaned toward me and returned the kiss. When we went back inside I told her about my mother's wedding, and Beverly asked to see me in the suit I'd bought for the occasion. So I put it on—a tan two-piece the color of toast—and she inspected me. She nodded, walking a circle. She approved of the suit. "You ought to dress up more often, Stanley—it makes a world of difference, believe me!" But she was dismayed by my shoes. "*Those?* You can't be serious. Oh, please. What are you thinking? Those are for a *postman.*"

"What's wrong with a postman?"

"Nothing—my father was a postman. But not in that suit!"

She insisted that we shop for shoes the next morning. It was rather late to go out for dinner, so I changed back into casual clothes and we called out for a pizza. Our order of a large Four Seasons (Beverly wanted to go easy on meat) turned out to be the biggest damn pizza I'd seen in my life. The delivery guy had to tilt the box sideways, to get it through the door.

We ate most of it, a cheese-gooey monster, and washed it down with a couple of bottles of red wine. We talked into the night and when we eventually retired at two-thirty A.M., our bodies heavy and stunned by all we'd consumed, Beverly surprised me. I'd slid into bed first and was already half dozing, assuming that the old rules for sleeping together still applied, when Beverly entered the room in a string panty and black lace bra. "Hey, Stan. What do you think?"

I sat up, blinking. I was in my undershorts and a Bernie T-shirt and suddenly felt very disoriented.

"Nice. Looks good."

She turned slowly, affording me a full view.

"It goes with the car interior," she said, giggling. "But I'll try it out there another time."

She leaned over to me—but just before our lips met, she jumped back again. "Wait a minute."

She bounced off the bed and out of the room.

A short time later she returned in another outfit, a lavender chemise with dangling garters. "How about this one, Stanley?"

"Great. It suits you very well." I hesitated, and then asked, "Are you saying that you've rejoined the club?"

"What do you mean?"

"You know what I mean. Sex."

She shrugged, and it was clear that I shouldn't have spoken in such a direct manner. Actually I'd preferred the first outfit, but Beverly was enjoying this, I could tell, so I encouraged her as I lay on my side and rubbed my stomach, caressing my pizza. "Anything else you'd care to show me?"

"Well, since you ask—" she said, and left the room.

It would've been madness to discourage her. On the other hand, I began to feel uneasy. Was I misreading her? Nothing wrong with Beverly getting a charge out of dressing up. Far from it. But now I wondered: is that all she intends to do? Maybe it's not the means to the end, but the end itself. Good Lord, this could be even more frustrating than the last time we slept together!

Next, a leather bodice and split panties. A point of no return, as far as I was concerned. This time I pounced. She let me, laughing ("But first you have to take off that awful T-shirt!" she said, pulling it over my head, tangling my arms). While I wrestled free, my hair standing on end with static electricity, she reached down and squeezed at the front of my undershorts. Beverly was no prude, once we got started. She pushed aside the blankets, and placed a pillow for optimum angle.

While all this was happening, I was conscious of many things. Conscious of the ways that she was different from Amy; conscious that this was something I'd always wanted from Beverly, but now that we were at it, my mind roamed and roved.

What next? I already wanted to know. Wondering, as I heard the urgent slap of our bodies, why does she trust me?

But such thoughts didn't last long. The savor of sensations became too strong—even if, before I was overwhelmed and entered forgetfulness, I knew that this would not be enough. And wasn't that what Beverly had said all along?

⟨⟨

THE NEXT morning Beverly escorted me in her Omega 600 to a mall where I bought a pair of Italian shoes. A strain on my credit card but a necessary investment, she reassured me. Soft leather, chocolate brown lace-ups. Beverly stood beside me in the mirror and exclaimed with pleasure at my feet. Her hand touched my waist, and she let it rest there. "See, Stanley? See the difference?" she said.

Afterward we went to an espresso house that she wanted to show me, a popular new place with soft jazz coming out of the ferns and precious curios screwed to the walls. It was a beautiful spring morning and we sat at a front window where we could enjoy the sunshine and a view of the parking area. (In case somebody tried to pull into a tight spot next to her new Omega 600.) I was wearing Reggie's sunglasses, the ones which he'd left on my dresser, and in my reflection in the window, I didn't look bad. Soon the conversation turned to my future.

"What next, then?" she asked. "Now that you've been laid off."

(She still didn't know the full story of my dismissal. Nor did I volunteer it.)

"Hard to say. I'm open to suggestions."

"You need to go someplace where the economy is moving. Frankly, I don't see why you left Chicago in the first place. How many people are there in that town you're at?"

My eyes had strayed to the front counter of the espresso house, where the manager, a young guy with a goatee and a black T-shirt, was ringing up an order. I thought: *Hell, I could do that job. He probably makes as much as I do.*

"About two thousand people, I guess," I told her.

"How much longer will you stay there?"

In a sudden vision I saw myself running a coffeehouse. My brother Riley could set me up. He had the money. What else did it take? Yes, my own place! A new beginning. If necessary, for business reasons, I could grow a goatee . . .

I fixed my eyes on Beverly. "Not much longer." I reached across the table and rested my hand on hers. It was hard to say what I meant by this combination of words and gesture. There was nothing thought out. It was more the situation, sitting in the coffeehouse with her, having this kind of conversation.

She smiled. "I wasn't trying to pry." Now she turned her gaze to the window and pretended to be interested in passersby. I observed Beverly's profile, her round cheek and pointy little nose, and she *was* pretty, in her sweet Beverly way. But now she removed her hand.

"This feels funny," I said. "I mean compared to last time. All of a sudden you seem different."

"No, I'm not. Not really." She hesitated. "But to tell you the truth, after the last time you came to see me, I didn't think I'd ever see you again. I thought you'd fall off the face of the earth. And if you did—I mean, if you'd fallen out of touch—well, then it would've been no great loss, frankly. Not for me."

This was a little confusing. "But you stayed in touch," I said.

"Yes. And you did, too. So I saw that there was more to you than I'd suspected. I like you but I'm not going to let anyone waste my time, Stanley. Last night was nice. But the ball's in your court, bub. You'd better not blow it."

At the counter, our order was called out, so I went to retrieve it. When I came back, I lowered Beverly's coffee in front of her.

"Did I freak you out?" she asked.

"No, you didn't freak me out. But I'm trying to think of the right thing to say. And—and I would like it to be something that would please us both. You believe me, don't you?"

"I want to," she said.

Then, for the rest of the morning, we spoke of other things.

☾

I CHANGED into my suit at Beverly's house, kissed her goodbye, and then I drove over to Riley and Serena's place. I arrived with plenty of time to spare. Our plan was to go to the town hall together for the wedding ceremony. When I entered their house, there was a great bustle of preparation.

"Hold still!"

"It hurts!"

"Stop it!"

Riley and Serena were trying to get their sons, Ryan and Justin, into their matching suits and ties and new spring shoes.

Before leaving, we were supposed to take pictures in the back-yard in front of the gazebo and lilacs. The boys' tiny suits were three-piece affairs, with smart paisley vests with side pockets and little watches on chains. When I saw these outfits, I didn't know whether to be impressed or depressed.

"You put your handkerchief in like that," Serena said. "*There.*"

A double-peaked fold. The paisley pattern matched the vest.

"Don't play with the watch," Riley scolded. "If you twist the chain it won't hang right."

During these instructions a young Salvadoran woman named Cristina rocked the boys' new baby sister, Ruthie, in her arms. Ruthie was running a temperature and she didn't cry, exactly; it was more like a soft, sad mewling.

"Where are the Q-tips?" Serena exclaimed, rushing forward, shaking Justin by the shoulder with one hand while her other hand held up a roaring blow-dryer. Her hair flagged sideways, as if from a hurricane sweeping through the house.

"Sorry?" said Cristina. She didn't catch the phrase.

"I'm hungry," said Ryan.

I offered to help but, to my relief, Riley said it would be better for me to stay out of the way. So I retreated to the den, sat back in a big comfortable chair and put my feet up. After a suitable pause to admire my shoes, I picked up a sports magazine and started to read.

Then Justin trotted in. I had the distinct impression that he was fleeing something. He picked up a remote control and, pointing it at a television in the bookcase, lit up the screen and began to flick through channels. The volume was very loud and he operated the remote control with an imperious snap of the wrist, like a lion tamer commanding tricks.

"Hey, could you turn that down?" I said. "Jeez."

He grunted. "All right, Speck." He altered the volume slightly.

"Call me Stanley. Uncle Stanley."

Now Serena swept in.

"There you are!"

She unscrewed a jar and held it out to him. Justin looked up, his thin lips wordless. Without protest he dipped his fingers and then, turning his attention back to the television, he applied the gel to his hair, plucking it into tufts.

"Ready?" Serena asked me.

After a photo shoot in the backyard, we piled into their family utility vehicle, a big-shouldered machine with massive tires that looked as if it could scale steep hills and the sides of office buildings. I noticed that Ryan had gel in his hair, too, and so did my brother Riley, though in his case the effect wasn't very successful because his hair was thinning, and the top of his scalp was an assembly of clotted clumps. On the other hand, who was I to judge? Even in my new suit and Italian shoes, I still felt like an unconvincing actor, an interloper. Soon-to-be-unemployed Stanley, the visiting country relative. When would he get a life? Who was tolerating whom?

The vehicle had three rows of seats: Serena occupied the front with Riley, the boys were strapped in the middle, and I sat in the far rear with Cristina and the baby Ruthie. My brother yelled out conversational bursts over his shoulder while accelerating across lanes with bold surges, weaving in and out of traffic with broad swipes of his forearm. Cars in his path risked being squashed like so many bugs.

"You gotta give Mom credit!" Riley shouted. "She doesn't give up, she just keeps coming back for more! Archie's all right, too, once you get to know him. You ought to see him flip pancakes."

This conversation was cut short when, next to me, the baby Ruthie became upset. She squalled, her face turned scarlet, and the soft spot on top of her head began to pulsate. It was alarming but then, as abruptly as it had started, the storm passed, Ruthie fell silent, and now she slobbered and wobbled and looked at me with molasses eyes. Her nanny Cristina flashed a smile at me and I attempted a conversation in Spanish, but she answered with such rapidity that I understood only a fraction of what she said, and then she became bored and let the conversation drop.

The town hall where the wedding vows would be exchanged was located in a steel-and-glass suburban civic center. According to the sign at the entrance, this place also housed a health club and meeting rooms for the Chamber of Commerce and Alcoholics Anonymous, as well as something called Positive Energy People. An odd mix of individuals mingled in the lobby, some in dresses and suits and ties, others in athletic gear and aerobics leotards. We followed arrows to the office of the Justice of the Peace, with Riley and Serena's boys running ahead like scouts while I choked back the schoolteacher's reflex of shouting, "Don't run!" Riley and Serena said nothing.

In the waiting room, I spotted my mother and went straight to her. She wore a long aqua dress with matching earrings, and she was chatting with a soldier, a very young man in uniform whose buzzcut hairstyle accentuated his protruding pink ears.

"This is Brandon," she told me, taking my arm and pulling me into the conversation. "He's getting married to Misty." She nodded toward a frizzy-haired young woman with too much makeup and a tight-lipped smile. She looked like someone from Legion's cheerleading squad. Technically she was legal, I supposed. "Archie's gone to see what's holding things up," my mother explained.

Apparently the Justice of the Peace was running behind schedule, and my mother had struck up the acquaintance of the young couple next in line. She appeared to be offering moral support. "This is a day you'll always remember! It's a celebration, don't be nervous." Handshakes were exchanged and the circle widened, and soon I found myself in conversation with a long-haired guy with piercings and a heavy metal T-shirt and thick-soled black boots.

"I'm Snooter," he told me. "I'm Brandon's witness."

"Hi. I'm her son." I pointed to my mother.

Snooter told me that Brandon's guard unit was shipping out to Iraq next week. "He's gonna get his ears full of sand," he chortled.

A city employee in a wheelchair whirred into the room, stopped abruptly, and then made a neat quarter-turn toward the crowd. He read aloud names from a clipboard. This was it: Brandon and Misty blinked, and then Brandon reached out and grabbed her hand with a convulsive movement. It seemed less affection than hanging on for dear life as she stepped forward with him, wide-eyed and pale, and their group headed out. I didn't see much of the couple after that because Snooter's big shoulders blocked my view, but Brandon's gesture and Misty's face went straight to my heart. *Good luck, kids,* I thought. *Better hold on tight.*

A smiling stranger advanced with an outstretched hand. "Stanley! So we meet at last! I've heard so much about you. You're a traveling man like me."

"Congratulations, Archie," I said.

He pumped my hand and patted my shoulder with his other hand. "I'm glad we can finally connect," I told him, and he laughed. Archie was wrinkled, with spiky eyebrows, but his handshake was firm and he had very white teeth for a man his age. My mother took his arm proudly.

"We hope to see more of you, Stanley. I'm so glad you've come back to America and settled down."

"How do you like retirement?" Archie asked.

This was puzzling. "What do you mean?"

It turned out that he was talking about baseball. "Do you miss the game?"

"It hasn't felt like retirement, I can say that much."

Archie slipped his arm around my mother's waist. "Our flight tomorrow leaves at the crack of dawn. In twenty-four hours we'll be lying on the beach!"

(Against my will I pictured him applying guava oils . . .)

"How do I look, getting married in white?" my mother asked.

Again, I was puzzled. Today, it seemed that I was behind on everything. My eyes moved along her aqua dress. Then she solved the riddle for me.

"My hair!" she exclaimed.

Everyone was laughing as the employee with the clipboard buzzed back into the room and called out their names. We trooped into a carpeted office and stood before the Justice of the Peace, a tall young woman who introduced herself as Melody Hardy. She read out her preliminary remarks from a spiral binder, *"Today in keeping with county code 36.15 of . . ."*

It was a simple business and lasted only a few minutes. Archie and my mother exchanged vows, and Melody sealed the deal. There would've been no further incidents, if not for me.

It was the strangest thing. Although a glitch was always possible, some accident or family screw-up—a problem with the kids, for instance—never once did I entertain the idea that *I* would be the culprit. Yet that's what happened. While listening to Melody Hardy read out the tired old formulas in an uninspired, bureaucratic tone to a group of people who were waiting to get it over with, I began to feel choked up. It came on quickly and was very peculiar. It's a cliché to cry at weddings but there it was, a tightening in my throat and a burning in my eyes. It was hard to control my breathing. What was happening? It couldn't be just the words. It couldn't be a sense of joy. It couldn't be the prospect of having Archie Morel as my stepfather. But, suddenly I felt pressed upon by all sides. By an accumulation of sensations. By time itself.

The generic quality of this pine-panelled room and fluorescent light fixtures were part of it—in their own fashion, they touched my heart. This office ceremony was so unlike the church weddings I'd attended as a child. The bareness and banality of this place somehow made the event more personal: there were no trappings to magnify the couple's intentions. My aging mother and Archie were what they were, exposed. So simple: she'd found someone to share her life with and had decided not to be alone. I looked at her, getting married "in white," as she said, and I felt a knot in my chest. Mixing with this sentiment were more unexpected images, of Brandon and Misty, this pair of young strangers, trying the same thing as my mother and Archie. Making promises. In a crazy sort of way it seemed the older couple was acting even more innocently than the kids. Hadn't they seen the world? What was their excuse? They ought to know better, for God's sake! But here they were, making promises, exposing themselves once more to the mocking disappointments of life.

My eyes filmed. *This is ridiculous, Stanley,* I thought. *For God's sake, what's the matter with you? Pull yourself together.* But I couldn't stop an upwelling of emotion. When Melody Hardy asked, "Does anyone know a reason why this union should not take place?" it was only rhetoric, she didn't expect an answer. Yet I could've called out, in all sincerity, "Sure, five or six, at least!"

Of course I didn't. I kept my eyes on the floor and took in deep breaths and tried to get a grip. Because the point was, despite five or six reasons, they were making promises anyway. They were still pushing themselves out there. That was the amazing part. Didn't they see? By what selection or convoluted process did they agree *not* to see? By what shared will? The tears flowed now and I wiped at them with the heel of my palm. I concentrated on controlling my breathing; it was like walking on a rope. Suddenly a sob escaped me, and people heard it. The moment was excruciating. Melody Hardy kept talking, my tears kept flowing; there was nothing I could do. A spring had been tapped. I gritted my teeth and made no more sounds because I didn't want to embarrass people, but I couldn't stop the flow. Actually, it was the first time I'd cried since my return to America. That was part of the problem, now, surely. What was the matter with me? I shouldn't have waited so long.

"Here, take this."

Serena reached around with a tissue. Her sons peered over the backs of their chairs, watching my every move, fascinated. Uncle Stanley looked like Uncle Nutball. I accepted the tissue and regained my composure for the rest of the speech, and a short time later excused myself and went to a toilet stall at the Civic Center, where I lost it entirely again. Sitting on the toilet seat in my suit, trying to keep it silent so the men using nearby stalls and urinals wouldn't hear me. It was a very strange Saturday afternoon. Unwinding the toilet paper, shaking all over, tears on my new shoes. What was this about? Archie was probably right: *You gotta connect.* But it seemed a terribly flawed set-up, like betting on Jim Snow to hit another home run. Who would take those odds?

I washed my face in the sink and went out to eat cake.

12

Wally liked to spend time in a small jungle of rhubarb that had sprung up on the east side of the house, lounging in the soft dirt or weaving his skinniness among the big, flat leaves. One sunny day, on a whim, I scooped him up and carried him over to my motorcycle and started the engine, still holding him by the scruff of the neck. His paws skittered for traction against the gas tank as I went once, twice around the yard. His yellow eyes bugged out at passing trees.

I stopped by the back door and turned off the engine and, when I released him, he shot through the air and disappeared into the rhubarb.

"Sorry, pal!" I called. "Bad idea."

Back at school, Mr. Worthington showed up at my class-room door one morning, gripping a little carton of orange juice, sucking on a straw. He beckoned to me. "Just a word, please."

In the hallway he told me in a low mumble that the super-intendent had advised the school board that my contract was "moot." Which meant, apparently, that I was out of danger of being sued. All I had to do was disappear discreetly. He sucked on his straw, gurgling. "Another thing, Stanley. There's that Ginny Rawlings business. We're going to need a write-up on her scholastic performance. Was she around for any of your last tests?"

"No, she wasn't."

"Oh. Too bad. Well, get something to me by the end of the week. Keep in mind the circumstances. The kid's had enough to deal with already."

When I pressed him about what he meant by a "write-up," it became clear that his request was different from the letter of recommendation that Amy had persuaded me to write for Ginny. He said that Mrs. Rawlings had contacted him to ask if we could validate Ginny's incomplete quarter and give her credit for the full academic year, because it would be tricky to enroll her in a private school at this late date. Maybe this was Amy's insurance policy, because Trilling Academy had rejected her daughter. Or maybe it was part of the same scheme. Who could say? Amy no longer communicated with me. At any rate, Mr. Worthington's request came with the clear implication that we should give her the benefit of the doubt.

So, a few days later, I submitted an exaggeratedly positive evaluation of Ginny Rawlings' work, full of praise for her promise, and advising that she should receive full credit for the year. For her missing test scores, I created a new column out of thin air: "Projected Outcome based on Potential." It was a pack of lies, mainly. Ginny had mountains ahead of her.

"Thanks, Stanley," Mr. Worthington said, glancing at it quickly. "This should be fine."

And so our spring cleaning had begun.

☙

"I was glad to get the roses," Beverly said. "The card was nice, too, but if I could make a suggestion, you'll need to try a little harder with the message."

This was the second time we'd spoken on the phone since my return from Chicago.

"Oh?"

"*Thinking of you.* Well, I get it, but thinking *what?* Do you see what I mean? This is the sort of thing I was telling you on Saturday. You know, when I said that the ball is in your court?"

"Yes."

"Well, this is where the fun begins. You're off to a passable start, Stanley, but you're going to have to keep sharp."

She laughed, but I was pretty sure that she wasn't joking. It made me nervous. It wasn't enough to do the right thing, you had to say the right thing. Beverly put considerable store in *words*. Or, it seemed, saying was another way of doing.

"I'd like to get some letters," Beverly continued. "Some good old-fashioned love letters, where you show some spark. The telephone is fine but a letter goes a long way. You can put in lots of things as long as you tell the truth. But don't try poetry unless you really know what you're doing. That gets dicey. Especially rhymes. I'm trying to help you out here, Stanley."

"I appreciate that."

I remembered the night that Beverly had tried on several outfits for me, and now I had the impression that I was doing something similar. What was necessary, I understood, was to find one that pleased her, and that I would feel comfortable in, too.

"Emails—well, you should know already, I don't want emails where you tell me what you had for lunch. And never, *ever* call me Bev."

"No way. Of course not. Unthinkable."

"I'm looking forward to this."

SHANA'S GIRLFRIEND Carol was stretching in her front yard when I got out of the Pontiac and came up the sidewalk. I hadn't known that she was back in town. She wore bright red running shorts, and lifted a leg behind her neck and held it there— long, tan, bent back like a grasshopper's. Clearly, Carol took her stretching seriously.

"Practicing for the circus?" I said.

"Nope. Getting ready for a run."

"Is Shana in?"

Now she lifted her other foot behind her neck. She balanced there. I could've rolled her away like a tire. From between her feet, her head spoke: "Yeah, she's out back."

So I walked around the house where I found Shana attaching a birdhouse to a clothesline pole. She manipulated a wire to tighten it down. "There," she said, with a twist of her pliers. "Does that look straight, Stanley?"

"Not bad."

"It's for bluebirds," she said, coming around to inspect the angle. "This way I can see it from my kitchen window. Now all I need is a bluebird." She went back and gave it a final adjustment. "What brings you here today?"

"I was wondering if you'd like to have a cat," I said.

Carol jogged by the fence, and we waved.

"I don't think so."

"Do you know anyone who would take him?"

She inquired as to why I was getting rid of Wally, which obliged me to reveal my plans to move to Chicago. "He doesn't really fit in the picture there. He's a country cat, all around."

"Why Chicago?" Shana asked. "What are you going to do there?"

Since I didn't care to talk about my contract, I referred vaguely to turning the page. She nodded and appeared unconvinced. It was true that my job prospects were uncertain and my earlier fantasy of running a coffeehouse sounded a little flighty; I'd have to come up with something better.

"Are you going there to be with someone?" she asked.

"Yes, I am, actually."

She smiled. "So. That says it right there."

"Yes. It does."

A few days later, Shana would do me the favor of getting the Snows to adopt Wally; but for now, just the way she smiled at me, implying complicity, was a boost. The plan was better for being aired. "Thanks," I added.

A short time later I bumped into Roy Heffernan at Jaycee's convenience store, pumping gas into his pick-up truck. He had a load of creosote posts, and told me that he'd finished putting in his garden. He offered me some tomato plants. I declined, saying that I was moving away soon, and then I mentioned that I was looking for a buyer for the Pontiac, since I wouldn't need a car in the city.

He was silent as he hung the nozzle back on the pump, and then screwed on his gas cap.

"I didn't think you'd last," he said, and then he went inside to pay.

❦

At first, my pupils ignored Ginny Rawlings' empty desk. They didn't ask about her, either. I didn't see any point in advertising the circumstances of her departure, though in a small town like Legion, surely word got round, even among kids. One day after lunch I caught Brody Bingham rifling through her desk to steal pencils, so when the final bell rang that afternoon, I decided to empty the desk of its contents. It was fairly crammed, and I realized that Ginny was a pack rat, which probably meant something, though I couldn't say what. In addition to textbooks that belonged to the school, which I returned to the storage shelves, there were old candy wrappers and the remains of a bag of cherry cough drops, smudged-up math worksheets from last fall, and old spelling tests still bleeding with my red ink. Buried at the bottom of this trash were some spiral notebooks in pristine condition, probably purchased for her at the beginning of the year, in anticipation of many labors. Their blank pages still smelled new. These notebooks I kept for myself.

The next day, for a class project, I asked my pupils to design a large fold-out greeting card for Ginny. "ALL THE BEST," it said, along with smaller doodles and jokes on pages opening out like an accordion. Given that they hadn't paid much attention to Ginny before, it was a little odd to lavish attention on her now; but everyone went along with the idea and no one complained, although some pupils wouldn't have bothered to sign it if I hadn't blocked the door when the bell rang for recess and made a simple bargain. You don't sign, you don't go outside.

Later that afternoon, Brain Rush interrupted in the middle of a lesson to ask, "What about Anita?" He cocked his thumb toward the guinea pig's cage.

"Huh? What about her?"

"Well, Ginny left her behind, right? Who gets her when school lets out? Can I have her?"

"I don't know. She doesn't belong to you."

He persisted, but I brushed him off. Later I overheard him telling another boy that it would be cool to do experiments on her.

So that pretty much ruled out *him* as a solution. Fortunately Ester Xicay agreed to take her. She liked to pick up the old demonstrator toothbrush from Dental Awareness Week, reach inside the cage, and scratch Anita's back with it. Anita purred and arched her spine, wanting more, blinking her moist black eyes.

☾

NELSON WAS philosophical as I tinkered with my motorcycle in the front yard. "You're letting me down but I won't say so. Just as long as you know."

Earlier, he'd groused about moving his stuff out of the meth house, but now that the last of the loading was done, he was in better spirits. Only one piece remained—his rocking chair—which we'd moved out onto the grass. He rocked under the blue sky and fleecy clouds as I told him, for the first time, the truth about my teaching contract. To my astonishment, none of my colleagues seemed to know yet, and I was beginning to suspect that Mr. Worthington had led me on with his story about the superintendent and the school board, just to make it easier to get rid of me. Otherwise, how could it remain a secret in this town?

"Oh, I don't think Worthington would lie about that," he said. "Word will get out, you'll be remembered as an impostor."

Nelson was probably my closest confidant in Legion—yet I had the impression that he took a certain pleasure in the ignominy of my exit.

"You going to spread the word?" I asked.

He shrugged. "Naw, why would I do that?" He rocked a little. "Patty Gordon will take care of it. But I could make up a bunch of weird shit, if you like. Just to keep people guessing."

"No thanks."

"So it's Chicago, then?" he asked. "You said you got family there. You'll be staying with them?"

"No, I got a place lined up."

The previous day, much to my surprise, Carol had taken the trouble to telephone me about a friend in Chicago who was offering a studio sublet. It was just for the summer but the price was good. She gave me the number, which I promptly called. Photos followed on the internet. In a matter of hours, we came to an agreement. The studio was located in Ravenswood, an easy jog up to Beverly's.

"You hear anything from your girlfriend?" he asked.

He was speaking, of course, about Amy; maybe he was goading me. I shook my head.

"I was talking to Crenshaw the other day," he said. "You know, the neighbor of the kid's grandma? She's out of the hospital now, and they look in on her."

"How is she?"

I was curious about Colleen.

"Well, the news is, there's some kind of plea bargain going on, for the son-in-law that attacked her, you know? It's not just his lawyers, either. Crenshaw says there's pressure from your girlfriend—"

"You know her name, Nelson. It's Amy. Just go ahead and say it, all right?"

"So, Amy is telling the mother that they can get a better deal with an out-of-court settlement. The trial would be a big hassle. Crenshaw was wondering if he and his wife might have to testify or something, but now it appears that the guy might not even go to trial. He could walk into another rehab, and that's that."

"Oh for Christ's sake. You're kidding me?"

"I wouldn't joke about that," he said, rocking.

"Drop it, Nelson. I don't want to hear any more."

It was all very twisted and confused. *A better deal.* To Amy it probably made perfect sense. I could hear her explaining that it was for Colleen's sake, and for Ginny's future. She would believe every word she said. She would be standing up for what was right, what was only fair. And me? I'd helped create this situation. Wasn't that a fine boast to make!

Nelson eyed me. "Are you still stuck on her?" he asked, with the hint of a grin on his lips.

"No, I'm not, Nelson. It was a big mistake. That's pretty obvious now."

"Uh huh."

The idea that he thought I was mooning over Amy was so off-putting that I announced to him that I'd found somebody else, a person with real potential, someone who was worth the trouble and uncertainty that life always brought. I told him about Beverly. He listened with a frown.

"I don't fucking believe it," he said eventually. "Oh, that's too easy. You're not kidding, are you? You leave this mess here, and then you run off to put your head on somebody else's lap! That's just the way. Nobody sticks around long enough anymore to construct something. Get a brain, Stanley. Are you just going to write us off? Do you hear yourself?"

Of course, I shouldn't have told him. "We're just getting started," I said, "nobody's counting on easy. I know—" And then the phone rang inside the house. I went in to answer and, as it happened, it was Beverly. I'd left her a message about the apartment in Ravenswood and this was our first chance to talk about it. I must've been on the line for at least twenty minutes before I hung up and went out to the yard.

Nelson, his chair and his van were gone.

That day was the last time I spoke to him.

𝐶

On the next Saturday afternoon I stepped out of the bank and saw Amy Rawlings. She was walking ahead of me in her pert, purposeful way, with a shoulder bag and a confident step, her head turning to look in store windows. I paused momentarily to allow her to put a greater distance between us, because I didn't want to overtake her, and then for half a block followed her, irresistibly watching her familiar form. My motorcycle was parked in front of Dwight's Diner and she was going in the same direction. No doubt she was in town to visit Colleen. Perhaps she'd dropped off Ginny at her grandmother's house. She stopped to look at the display window of Antiques and Collectibles. She looked back and saw me approaching, and she smiled. My first reaction was to slow down, but now she stepped in my direction.

"What's the matter, Stanley? Don't you want to be seen with me?"

"Never mind what I think."

She frowned. "Maybe you forget that we could still be friends."

"Is that so?"

She wore a smart blue jacket, and boots that made her taller. An unfamiliar pair of glasses hung around her neck on a fine chain and she ran her fingers up and down the chain as we conversed. She tilted her head, smiling. "Anyhow, Stanley—how are you?"

"Good. How are Colleen and Ginny?"

"Doing better, thank you for asking. Colleen's back on her feet. Ginny appreciated the card." She waited for me to say something else, but I didn't. This was the moment to seize: I should have continued walking. I felt it in my gut. But I didn't move.

"Mr. Worthington has been a peach," she continued, "he's arranged for Ginny to get full credit for the school year. And with your letter of recommendation, she stands a good chance of getting into Trilling Academy next fall. We just have to work out a few details."

"What's going to happen with Reggie?" I asked.

She gave a dismissive puff. "We're finished," she said. "Obviously."

She went on to confirm the out-of-court settlement that Nelson had alluded to, and she added, "He's going to be in treatment for a while, and he should thank his lucky stars that he's not in jail. He's at a residential facility in Urbandale. They've got sports therapy there, running and biking, along with the counseling, and he's working on a personal memoir. He's up to 100 pages." She paused, waving at an older woman across the street. "I let go of Tivoli's. It was a good experience but it ran its course. Now I'm an assistant with the County Board of Supervisors."

"The what?"

"It's actually quite interesting. Reggie's uncle Nathan—that's on his mom's side—he's on the board and they've decided to ask me to help out. When Nathan steps down I might even replace him, who knows? It doesn't sound glamorous but I'm learning all kinds of stuff, Stanley, I've been reading up. They need new blood. You know there's no state better placed than Iowa in the fight against world hunger? We've got the best of

America's resources, right here. We just have to harness our assets. Midwesterners are by nature too modest and we sell ourselves short."

Did she really believe this, too? I think so. And then we were interrupted by the woman from across the street who'd come to inquire about Colleen's condition. I left them there on the town square, as she offered Amy her sympathy and support.

❧

I PUT out a jar in the yard to make sun tea. The trees were in full leaf, my grass needed cutting. School had been out for several days and I'll always remember the pause, the thick silence, the queer ghostliness of it all as I stood and looked around my cleared-out classroom before going down to the office to turn in my keys. Who was next? Who would remember any of this?

Now I was experiencing a similar pause as I considered the meth house and the surrounding fields. How much longer would it be? I was still waiting for my last paycheck.

On an impulse I left the yard and walked through the orchard and climbed the fence, wondering about the state of the river. I hadn't seen it up close for weeks and I wanted to see if the water had cleared up, or if there was still visible sludge and clumpy green algae.

It wasn't with the thought that "This is The Last Time Before I Go." Yet I was aware of the possibility. Maybe it was the "Next-to-Last Time." In any case, it was with a sense of leave-taking.

I started down the slope till I reached the edge of the woods. Birds twittered above, and sunbeams shot spokes of light through the branches. The ground was still damp in places but generally the softness of spring had surrendered to the firmness of summer. Walking here now was like the first

– 202 –

time I'd set out from the meth house to explore the area. I stepped over a fallen log and flushed a rabbit which bounced through the undergrowth.

A first glimpse of the river, silver through the brush. And then, from behind me, I heard the sound.

Clong! Clong! Clong!

I stopped, turned around.

Clong! Clong!

Strange. It was coming from my house. But that didn't make sense. The bell was ringing in the orchard—but that wasn't possible. There was no clapper. So how could it ring? I turned around and started back through the trees.

Clong! Clong!

When I came into the field, sloping up toward the orchard, I saw someone standing on the fence, reaching up with a stick to beat the bell. Two other figures walked along the wires, and waved. As I drew closer, I saw that it was the Snows, and now Jim climbed down from the fence.

What were they doing here?

A few days ago, when I'd stopped by their place to drop off Wally, I'd spoken only to Mrs. Snow. She'd said that the kids were off riding their bikes somewhere. "My, how they get around," she told me, as we stood in the front yard and I opened the cardboard box and Wally sprang out with quivering limbs, casting me a reproachful look as he ventured across the unfamiliar grass. Mrs. Snow and I conversed briefly but she seemed a shy woman, tugging at the sleeve of a sweater that she wore despite the warm day. "We used to have a dog but it disappeared," she told me. I thanked her for taking Wally and left, with a sense that there was still something more to be said.

"Hello," I called as I approached the children. "Everything okay?"

"We saw you in the field when we were on the road. We thought you would hear the bell," Christine explained.

She smiled shyly and I could tell by the way Jim hung back that his sister had put him up to climbing the fence and hitting the bell. And what I'd assumed was a stick in his hand was actually my unused curtain rod, which he must've found in the grass. Billy Snow stood behind him, but I didn't get a good look at his face because of the visor on his cap, and because a cricket had just hopped near his feet and he was studying the ground, trying to spot it again.

"What can I do for you?" I asked.

"We wanted to thank you for the cat," she said. "Miss Linn said you were going away. We brought you some strawberries."

This took me aback, but I went to the corner post and climbed the fence and joined them on the other side. "I should be thanking you," I said. "You're the ones doing me a favor."

On the way back to the house Billy ran ahead and Jim swished the rod at passing weeds. When we reached the yard, I saw their bicycles lying in the grass. Billy bent over one, and began untying a plastic bag attached to the handlebars. "Don't spill them!" Christine called.

At first I was going to invite them into the house, but the sun was pleasant and it seemed like too nice a day to go inside. "I can't say no to strawberries, but won't you help me eat them? That would be better than eating them alone."

They didn't require much persuading, though they preferred juice to tea. We spread out a cloth and improvised a picnic on the grass. I wondered if they'd come on their own initiative, or if their mother had put them up to this; but, in any case, the simple fact that they'd bothered to ride here impressed me. We conversed about Wally and about other pets; they told me about their dog and experiences with rabbits. "We used to have a turtle," Christine said. "But it ran away." There was a pause, and then they burst out laughing. Apparently they shared this joke. When Billy laughed, he had a surprisingly deep voice for his age. "*Stop it,*" Jim told him, because in his enthusiasm Billy had picked up the rod and was swinging it around, playfully but wildly.

"I'm glad you stopped by today," I said. "I appreciate this. It's true I'm leaving soon. This is very kind."

Christine smoothed the cloth in front of her, rising to her knees, and brought a strawberry to her lips. "There was still time," she said.

I looked out across the yard to the rolling fields beyond, the curve of the horizon. "Yes," I said slowly. "There's still time."

Jim looked up. "Why did you come here?"

I wasn't ready for this question. Lately, people tended to ask where I was going. But it was an important question. If I'd been quicker in my understanding of things, I would've replied with a sweeping gesture toward this spot of green, their gift of strawberries, toward Christine and Billy and Jim himself, and said, "For this." But at that moment, I didn't know how to put this world into words.

But even if I couldn't say it, in my heart I felt the truth. Whoever or whatever we were was only a moment of such pain and pleasure as we clung to the side of the earth.